LEGACY

Bone Frog Bachelor Series

Book Four

SHARON HAMILTON

SHARON HAMILTON'S BOOK LIST

SEAL BROTHERHOOD BOOKS

SEAL BROTHERHOOD SERIES
Accidental SEAL Book 1

Fallen SEAL Legacy Book 2

SEAL Under Covers Book 3

SEAL The Deal Book 4

Cruisin' For A SEAL Book 5

SEAL My Destiny Book 6

SEAL of My Heart Book 7

Fredo's Dream Book 8

SEAL My Love Book 9

SEAL Encounter Prequel to Book 1

SEAL Endeavor Prequel to Book 2

Ultimate SEAL Collection Vol. 1 Books 1-4 /2 Prequels

Ultimate SEAL Collection Vol. 2 Books 5-7

SEAL BROTHERHOOD LEGACY SERIES
Watery Grave Book 1

Honor The Fallen Book 2

Grave Injustice Book 3

Deal With The Devil Book 4

BAD BOYS OF SEAL TEAM 3 SERIES
SEAL's Promise Book 1

SEAL My Home Book 2

SEAL's Code Book 3

Big Bad Boys Bundle Books 1-3

BAND OF BACHELORS SERIES

Lucas Book 1

Alex Book 2

Jake Book 3

Jake 2 Book 4

Big Band of Bachelors Bundle

BONE FROG BROTHERHOOD SERIES

New Year's SEAL Dream Book 1

SEALed At The Altar Book 2

SEALed Forever Book 3

SEAL's Rescue Book 4

SEALed Protection Book 5

Bone Frog Brotherhood Superbundle

BONE FROG BACHELOR SERIES

Bone Frog Bachelor Book 0.5

Unleashed Book 1

Restored Book 2

Revenge Book 3

Legacy Book 4

SUNSET SEALS SERIES

SEALed at Sunset Book 1

Second Chance SEAL Book 2

Treasure Island SEAL Book 3

Escape to Sunset Book 4

The House at Sunset Beach Book 5

Second Chance Reunion Book 6

Love's Treasure Book 7

Finding Home Book 8

Sunset SEALs Duet #1

Sunset SEALs Duet #2

LOVE VIXEN

Bone Frog Love

SHADOW SEALS

Shadow of the Heart

Shadow Warrior

SILVER SEALS SERIES

SEAL Love's Legacy

SLEEPER SEALS SERIES

Bachelor SEAL

STAND ALONE BOOKS & SERIES

SEAL's Goal: The Beautiful Game

Nashville SEAL: Jameson

True Blue SEALS Zak

Paradise: In Search of Love

Love Me Tender, Love You Hard

ABOUT THE BOOK

Former Navy SEAL billionaire Marco Gambini and his forever love, Shannon, are back together again after a harrowing rescue of Marco's advance team in Africa, threatening to cancel their long-planned wedding at the Pink Palace owned by the Sultan of Bonin.

He has hosted the Sultan and his entourage for a month, and now they leave to return home to their Indian Island kingdom, to prepare for the big wedding. Plans for building the housing project in West Africa are on hold, temporarily, while they ready themselves for the biggest adventure of their lives: their wedding day.

That is, if the bad guys and dangerous militia in Africa will leave them alone. Armed with vengeance and hatred, the terrorist group plans the ultimate revenge, putting more than just Marco's company in jeopardy. They attempt the unthinkable.

Only Marco and his team are up to the task of not only saving their special day, but preserving a dying man's legacy.

AUTHOR'S NOTE

I always dedicate my SEAL Brotherhood books to the brave men and women who defend our shores and keep us safe. Without their sacrifice, and that of their families—because a warrior's fight always includes his or her family—I wouldn't have the freedom and opportunity to make a living writing these stories. They sometimes pay the ultimate price so we can debate, argue, go have coffee with friends, raise our children and see them have children of their own.

One of my favorite tributes to warriors resides on many memorials, including one I saw honoring the fallen of WWII on an island in the Pacific:

> "When you go home
> Tell them of us, and say
> For your tomorrow,
> We gave our today."

These are my stories created out of my own imagination. Anything that is inaccurately portrayed is either my mistake, or done intentionally to disguise something I might have overheard over a beer or in the corner of one of the hangouts along the Coronado Strand.

I support two main charities. Navy SEAL/UDT Museum operates in Ft. Pierce, Florida. Please learn about this wonderful museum, all run by active and former SEALs and their friends and families, and who rely on public support, not that of the U.S. Government. www.navysealmuseum.org

I also support Wounded Warriors, who tirelessly bring together the warrior as well as the family members who are just learning to deal with their soldier's condition and have nowhere to turn. It is a long path to becoming well, but I've seen first-hand what this organization does for its warriors and the families who love them. Please give what your heart tells you is right. If you cannot give, volunteer at one of the many service centers all over the United States. Get involved. Do something meaningful for someone who gave so much of themselves, to families who have paid the price for your freedom. You'll find a family there unlike any other on the planet. www.woundedwarriorproject.org

CHAPTER 1

"THEY ARE LOVELY to look at, aren't they, Marco?" the Sultan of Bonin asked me.

He was dressed in a bright white cotton tunic with gray slacks beneath. I wondered if he had ever owned a pair of real leather shoes, because I only saw him in sandals or flip-flops. And in Florida, it was always flip-flops, the brighter the better.

Shannon was at the shoreline splashing water with all of the ladies from the sultan's harem joining in. They were laughing and acting like a bunch of school girls, completely oblivious to protocol, customs, or any danger that might lurk in the shadows. It was a brief reprieve in an otherwise very dangerous year, but we were headed to the altar, come Hell or high water. I greatly looked forward to the lavish wedding at the Pink Palace, complete with a pink beach in the sultan's private island kingdom on invitation and organized by him and his incredible family.

I'd been looking forward to it since the evening Shannon agreed to marry me, this old bucket of bones, former Navy SEAL, former multi-billionaire, but now just a billionaire. And that was good enough for her, so it was good enough for me. I'd been doing a lot of adjusting these days.

For the first time in my life, I wasn't kicking and screaming along the way. I was choosing a higher path, perhaps, and looking for contentment, even though I was a man of action.

Never had I ever thought this could happen.

I was getting married for the *rest* of my life, which meant forever.

"They are just that, aren't they?" I said. "Angels, sent here to bring us both multitudes of pleasure and satisfaction, making our lives richer and full of magic."

He grumbled a deep guttural chuckle, nodding. "Agreed."

"I don't think I've ever seen Shannon so happy. Your wives are marvelous guests. I was trying to show you what our life is like here, but your ladies have transformed this place—so unfamiliar—with their joy. They have made such an impact on the whole area. They bring their own magic, and here I thought it was Florida. They are going to take home a part of the Florida Gulf Coast with them."

I studied his eyes as he focused on the women

down below our balcony. His nod was barely perceptible. His breathing was a bit ragged, his eyes a little droopy, but other than that, no one would suspect the man was gravely ill.

"A gift for a dying man? Would you say that?"

"No, Sultan. I didn't mean that at all."

"Ah, but I took it that way. It is unfortunate that we have to die. But if we are to die, we should all be so lucky as to die happy, like I am."

"Truer words were never spoken, my sultan."

"In my case, it actually is fortunate to know that I have little time left. I am grateful to be able to spend the last days of my life planning a wedding for you and Shannon. It's like a bit of me will always be with you as long as you are together, because I'm helping to create that memorable bond between you by hosting you at my palace. I am going to be forever grateful. And long after I'm gone, I'm hoping your wedding will be the talk of the kingdom."

My Navy SEAL training kicked in on red alert. I had only allowed myself to shed a tear a handful of times. It was usually at funerals for one of my teammates or one of their close family members. But the sultan's strong words hit me in the solar plexus, throwing me off balance for a moment, and before long, I felt the moisture in my eyes threatening to spill over and run down my cheeks. I inhaled deeply and willed my eyes to clear.

Most of the time, I could make it hold back.

This time, it worked.

"My friend, if this in any way is going to shorten your life, you know I would call a halt to it. A significant portion of the work will be done by others, but if I get any inkling that this is going to be hard on you physically, I must insist that we postpone or conduct the ceremony elsewhere so that it's not so taxing to you. But I understand, even if it was so, you would probably lie to me and make me believe that it wasn't."

He had a sparkle in his eye as he looked up at me, smiled, and then returned his gaze to the women.

"I didn't use to be so transparent, Marco. You've changed that in me as well. It's funny how life teaches you, as it's slipping away, what's really important. Our bodies go away, our soul transports, and what remains, what's truly important, are the memories and the friendships and the love we've created. You can't participate in that if you don't *feel*. And part of that extreme connection and feeling creates pain. There's no way to avoid it, is there?"

I doubted I had changed him as much as my association with him had changed me. He was far more to me now than just my client, my sometimes investor or benefactor. "Friendship" didn't do it justice. Even "family" didn't describe it fully. If I wasn't careful, I'd start bawling like a baby.

I locked my jaw and cleared my throat.

"You mean loss, my sultan?"

"Yes. I used to want to be famous, planned to get richer and richer as the years went by, wanted to have the jewels and gold fall from my fingers like rain and watch others squeal with joy at being given some of my kingdom's bounty."

He stopped. So I had to ask him.

"And now? What's changed?"

"Now, from where I'm sitting, I'm just enjoying being a beach bum in a multi-million-dollar house rented by my friend." He smiled at this, placing his arm on my shoulder with a smile. "And my desire is that I will leave a big hole. That I will be missed, not thought of as successful, leaving his kingdom in good shape or growing his wealth, assets, children, families, taking on more wives. I just want to be *missed*."

"You will be. I guarantee it. I know Shannon and I will miss you."

I wrestled my wits back into that cool, deadly column of steel that could defeat anything, including death. I continued in a new vein.

"But I don't want to talk about those times. I have no idea how many years I have myself. None of us do. But I want to spend whatever time we do have together living, not watching each other die. Because we die a little bit every day, don't we?"

He frowned, again nodding. His eyes had filled with water he didn't try to cover up.

"Yes. Even the children. Even the most beautiful and coveted wither and die, sometimes fast. But it is an adventure we can never escape."

I was feeling morose suddenly, even with the idyllic laughter and the sounds of splashing water below us. There was nothing I could do to stop the passage of time, the inevitable that was going to befall all of us. I didn't like the idea of having something taken away from me, even though I knew we couldn't hold on to everything, especially as we were leaving this world. But the feeling of being vulnerable and not able to control the end—to have a say in it but not really be able to control it—that was difficult for me.

I'd always prided myself on having such excellent control over all my business activities. Yet, over the past two years, life had been the most difficult, with the divorce from Rebecca, the bombing of my office building, and almost losing Shannon. The world still was a dangerous place, and I knew, even here at the Gulf Coast of Florida, danger lingered. I would have to be vigilant in my protection of this special family.

I had something I'd wanted to speak to him in private since his arrival in Florida for his first-ever vacation in Florida. Probably his last.

"As long as we are talking about futures and spending our time in the living side of the ledger, I wanted to ask you why you don't consider building your housing projects in some location other than those war-torn areas in Nigeria. I know you purchased the property, made promises. I know you've invested quite a bit already."

I was worried how he'd take my question, but I had no option now but to continue.

"Don't you think there are other places you could build where you could do good and where your legacy would have a chance of standing for longer than just a few months or years?"

"I want to build it for those people because of how those people have suffered. Everything they've had has been taken away from them. Even their culture has been robbed of them, shredded by evil men doing unspeakable things."

"But what's the point of building something the militia groups are just going to bomb and tear apart? What's the point of making people see there is good and hope in the world and then have them experience everything being destroyed and taken away again? Maybe that part of the world is so overrun with hate and these competing groups that it can't be fixed for a century, many years. Perhaps it's too soon to do this. Shouldn't we have peace first? Order? Remove the chaos?"

"Ah, I anticipated this, Marco. I knew this question was coming."

He wasn't smiling this time, and I knew I was cruising close to the edge of what he would accept hearing.

"What's the benefit in just adding fuel to the bonfire?" I asked him.

"You mean my project becomes a new target for them to attack?"

"Yes. Exactly. I mean, why do it there?"

"Because it's what I can do. I can try and make a difference."

"But don't you suppose there are other places where you could do good and it would last? Do you have to take it to absolutely the most dangerous place in the world? Don't get me wrong, Sultan. I will build your project anywhere you say you want to, but I question whether it's worth the risk to your sons, since your legacy may not survive the attack. Your boys could be hurt or worse."

"Am I to assume, Marco, that you have lost some of your nerve?"

"No, sir. It's not my nerve. I've gained more knowledge. It's just hit me plain as day that I think it's a mistake to build it in Nigeria. I can teach your boys building projects and how to run big companies here in Florida or some other place in the United States where the experience would be much different than Africa, and you could do good."

"But this is the land of opportunity, the land of plenty. I wanted to give something to people who don't have that. Who have nothing to live for."

I thought very carefully for several minutes before I spoke. I knew I was about to make a huge shift in our priorities. I needed to make this point to him.

"My sultan, I'm going to show you some people who have lost everything."

I drove the two of us in my red Bentley convertible with the top down. We were the picture of opulence and abundance. With the sunshine on our faces, the warm Florida gulf breeze rearranging our hair, and wearing matching Aviators sunglasses, we were spending a day few other people on the planet got to experience. We were lucky. Yes, I admit I felt entitled too.

We scooted down Gulf Boulevard and turned onto the causeway crossing the dark blue waters of Tampa Bay. We were headed east away from the Gulf. After several minutes of complete silence, we finally pulled off the highway and onto a side street that led to the complex I wanted to visit. At a stoplight, we heard the surrounding noises of cars, blaring country music, the barking of talk radio soaring to the heavens, construction work, sirens, businesses, and airplanes. In the middle of all of that, he turned to me and asked, "Where are we going, Marco?"

He trusted me, but he did appear slightly worried. I knew he didn't like hospitals. I anticipated this.

"I'm going to show you something you've never seen before. You're going to have to trust me on that. It's safe, but I'm going to show you something that you're never going to forget."

When the light changed, we turned into a complex shaded by enormous trees on both sides of the roadway with trunks that were five or more feet in diameter, interspersed with palm trees and grassy knolls and walkways. We passed a large cemetery with two navy blue tents readying for a funeral, American flags flying opulently everywhere we looked.

The setting was gorgeous. Old sandstone-colored buildings with tile roofs looked like they could have been built for a Spanish garrison. The entire complex had been built probably prior to World War II, the quarters resembling those I'd stayed at in Hawaii at Pearl Harbor. Newer buildings had been built and added to the main halls, and as we headed down the street, we stopped in front of a large brand-new hospital several stories high, sparkling like a diamond in the sunlight in front of us. A huge American flag flew in the lawn in front of the parking lot that almost dwarfed the building itself. Several smaller flags, depicting the different branches of service and the State of Florida, stood nearby, as witness to the greatness of our flag.

I was filled with pride.

In his white tunic, his starched and pressed sandstone slacks, and his bright orange flip-flops, he followed me with short stubby steps, gripping the bronze handrails, until we climbed the four concrete stairs to the main lobby. Adjacent the stairway was a ramp, bordered with handrails on both sides for the sick or disabled.

Inside, elevator music played. The steel-colored travertine floor was inlaid with scrolling flowers on vines, butterflies, and several eagles. It echoed noisily and reflected every little bit of activity in the enormous rotunda we were standing in. An information desk at one end of the hall gave us the guidance I needed.

I made my inquiry and then took the sultan's arm, and we walked down the center corridor and around the corner to a special laboratory I'd helped fund.

"This is a government facility?" he asked.

"It's the Veteran's Administration Hospital. This is where they treat our wounded servicemen, mostly those who are residents of Florida and other Southern states. They are some of the best doctors and technicians in the world here, and I want you to see what they do. I have helped fund a new orthotics lab, something I'm very proud of. It was out of working with these people that my vision for the Trident Towers was born."

I could see his eyes squint, but his skepticism appeared to be waning.

I opened the frosted glass door, etched with the Trident logo of my company. Once inside, we saw machinery, drills, saws, and equipment dangling from cords hung from the ceiling. Tables were strewn with artificial parts, from flesh-colored prosthetic hands to forearms, legs, ankles, and toes. There was a casting room. Someone polished a metal brace with a grinder that let out a high-pitched squeal that almost hurt my ears. I could smell some of the polymer and plaster materials that they used. Several other technicians were assembling components for artificial limbs. They tested and examined their handiwork, bent the artificial knees, and moved the artificial ankles and feet slowly to adjust for anything that was needed.

Looking over at the sultan, who I had nearly forgotten was there, I saw his eyes widen and his jaw drop. The overall effect on him was greater than I thought it would be. He was clearly in shock.

I spotted someone I wanted to visit with, so I directed us to walk to the other end of the room where a gentleman in a wheelchair had just returned from a private, curtained dressing area. The man was missing both legs, one arm, and part of the right side of his face and ear, obvious to most people that he'd been a victim of a bomb blast of some kind.

The orthotist he was working with was fitting him for an arm to give him more mobility, and I was privy to the fact that he would also be fitted with two legs. I had taken a special interest in this young Navy man because he had, like me, passed his BUD/S training, but he needed to serve one more rotation before he could complete the rest of his SEAL training, and was injured before he could finish.

I had given him one of my gold Tridents on a visit earlier in the year, and he wore it proudly on his T-shirt.

"Hey, Sam, nice to see you again," I said to the young lieutenant.

"Marco! This is going to be a great day. I come in with just one appendage, and I'm going to leave with two. Soon I'll have all four. God-willing, I can begin to run again! That's pretty good, don't you think?"

He was still handsome even though the skin around his eye was shriveled and scarred. He'd lost his ear, but luckily not his vision. His smile was slightly crooked, but it gave him character and didn't bother me one bit.

"Hell yeah, it's a good day. Any day we're alive is a good day."

We fist-bumped our lefts.

"I have someone I want you to meet, Sam. This here is the Sultan of Bonin, a friend of mine, who is also hiring me to build a housing project. I came to show him some of the work we're doing here, and I wanted him to meet a real-life hero."

Sam grinned from ear to ear, extending his left hand instead of his non-existent right and shook hands with the sultan awkwardly. "Nice to meet you, sir. You'll have to forgive me, but I don't know where your kingdom is. Where is Bonin anyway?" he asked.

"It's a tiny island inside the Indian Ocean. Independent of India, but very dependent on trade with her. Our kingdom used to have several other islands, more like atolls, but India has taken them back. I have the best and the largest of the bunch."

He smiled and released Sam's hand carefully.

I noticed the sultan suddenly squinting a bit as the technician removed the sheet covering young Sam's leg stumps where he'd been surgically repaired just below both hips. This also exposed a very scarred upper arm and a small pointed fleshy protrusion at the end of the stump instead of an elbow joint. That protrusion was being fitted into a plastic custom-formed cast and strapped with Velcro straps around his chest and crisscrossing down his back for support.

Sam was attempting to move the arm but hadn't

quite figured out how to do so. It stiffly sat on the edge of his chair and then into his lap. He attempted to reach the table and pick up a pen, which quickly dropped. The technician was patient, working with him to adjust the prosthesis so he could control the movements more efficiently.

The sultan's eyes were transfixed on the young Navy lieutenant. I could see he wanted to ask questions.

"Go ahead. Ask him anything you like," I blurted out.

"Thank you, Marco. Were you involved in a bomb blast or what caused this unfortunate accident?"

"Yes, we were broadsided by a fishing boat carrying arms to the enemy. Part of the armaments blew up while we were trying to offload people to safety. The boat had drifted without a motor, and we had picked up a distress call, but they had decided to scuttle our ship or try to take us all hostage, which didn't work, but some of us were injured in the process."

"Tell him, Sam, where it happened," I asked him.

"Off the west coast of Africa, below the bulge." Sam shifted between the sultan's eyes and mine, sensing there was some significance to my question. And indeed it had the effect I was looking for.

I knew from conversations with Sam that he had considered suicide. He was regretting seeing his family and initially didn't want them to visit, but when his girlfriend finally came to Germany, his attitude about living began to change as well. It was that little taste of honey he needed to get him back on track. I wasn't going to reveal his private life, perhaps saving it for when I had full permission. So I improvised.

"Sam and I have spent a lot of time talking about all this. It was through my acquaintance with him that I discovered veterans needed equipment, and they were not getting this from the federal government. In response, we set up a grant that I underwrote so I could donate to the hospital. They could get their equipment, and it didn't raise the conflict of government-private partnership. I'm very proud of this clinic, because it's one of the best in the whole United States."

"I had no idea, Marco, but this is so like you. Never leave anybody behind, right?"

"Hooyah, S.O. Gambini!" Sam boomed, raising his left hand in a fist.

As we walked away, the sultan kept looking back, watching Sam and his orthotist work on the arm. Each time Sam caught his gaze and waved, the sultan smiled a little more.

"These are the people who have come home after doing their duty, who gave more than just their time. They left part of their bodies behind on the battlefield. They were injured by men of pure evil, and this is the least I can do for them."

"I understand now, Marco."

"These are really the people who have nothing."

CHAPTER 2

THE WOMEN HAD congregated around the swimming pool after their morning frolic in the ocean, several of them braiding each other's hair or painting toes and fingernails. A couple of the younger wives were dancing to Western music—or at least attempting to dance to Western music, which was something totally unfamiliar to them.

Shannon had just dipped in the water to cool off and was handed a large beach towel by the sultan's number one wife.

"I have something I've wanted to show you ever since I got here. Would you come up to my bedroom please?" the attractive older woman, the first of his wives, asked.

"Of course. Let me continue to dry off, and then I'll)e right up there."

"I'll wait," she quipped with a wink.

As Shannon dried off, three other wives approached, requesting permission to accompany them. Not having a clue what this was all about, Shannon agreed after glancing at the older woman.

"This is all very mysterious," she said to the wives.

Most of what Shannon got back were titters and giggles. They were such a tight-knit group that each of them was extremely involved in everyone else's life. Gossip was commonplace, and it was more a communal relationship, a true sisterhood rather than some kind of competitive show for the sultan's attention. They didn't try to belittle each other or encourage his advances too obviously, being very conscious of their sister wives' feelings. Shannon was fascinated with the whole makeup of their arrangement.

With the towel slung around her waist, she slipped on her sandals and followed the older woman upstairs to the bedroom.

She was instructed to sit on the edge of the bed while the older woman and two others opened the massive closet doors and brought out five large cardboard boxes. When the lid was removed on the first box, Shannon could now see what the purpose of the meeting was all about. Pulled from inside each box, delicately draped over well-tanned arms and freshly painted pink, red, and purple fingernails, were yards and yards of beautiful silk saris. Some were edged with ribbons of silver and gold, glistening in the noonday sun. The bright, vibrant colors of turquoise, purple, fuchsia, reds, and oranges were almost a shock to the system. In the Florida atmosphere, the brilliant colors seemed to fit very well.

She was encouraged to stand as the wives busied themselves wrapping her in the beautiful silks, including trying several different saris for her head and around her shoulders as a shawl for windy weather. Some were wrapped strapless or over one shoulder, designed for warmer climates. The wives drew out over thirty beautiful hand-made saris. Marco had told Shannon that often these works of art could cost many thousands of dollars.

The hand stitching and detail, applique, and patchwork designs of exotic flowers, birds, and vine blossoms of all colors splashed across the silks, nearly giving her a headache. She was in complete awe.

His number one wife commanded, "So your job is to choose which ones of these are your favorites. I'm giving these to you as a gift. You choose as many as you like. Your wedding is to be a feast that will continue for several days, and you will need morning saris. You will need afternoon tea saris, and you will need romantic saris for midnight walks on the beach. You are going to need many, many costumes, and it is our custom that wearing the same sari twice during your wedding week is bad luck for the marriage. So you wear them each one time. Then you fold them up, and we pass them on."

Shannon was embarrassed with the opulence and the generosity of the women in front of her.

"These are stunning. I don't know what to say. I've never seen such beautiful fabric and such vibrant colors. I'm so afraid to wear them, that I'll spill something on them—and I know they can cost a small fortune. I truly don't deserve such a gift."

"Nonsense, dear Shannon. Just like when we made you up to dress as a dancing girl, to be alluring for your husband, it is our job to make sure you make a stunning entrance, that you are the center of all the attention, that you wear robes fit for a queen. Because you are a queen. You're Marco's queen."

"I am speechless. Thank you." Shannon hugged each of the women one by one. "I feel like I'm going to need a dolly or a crane to bring back some of these. These are simply amazing."

The sultan's first wife chuckled. "We will bring them back with us after you choose today. You'll see them again on the island for your big day, and they will be washed and pressed and prepared for you—scented, of course—so that you don't have to travel with them. But we do need to narrow it down. Otherwise, all these boxes, we're going to use all of them. You'll see. You can go through quite a few."

One of the younger wives added, "And Marco is not to see you wear any of these prior to the wedding day, which is why we are showing them to you today. You are not to allow a man's eyes to fall upon you when you wear these gowns, or it is again considered bad luck for your marriage."

It took Shannon all of two minutes to remove her bathing suit and put on the silk slip undergarment they gave her. One by one, they tried on nearly all the saris in the boxes, setting aside certain ones as a definite yes, placing some on the other side of the bed when they couldn't decide, and a third pile for saris that Shannon didn't particularly care for color-wise, but the wives were going to try to overrule her decisions.

The women worked like bees, wrapping and un-wrapping, examining folds, tying sashes, layering and positioning the precious silks.

"And we haven't even gotten to the jewelry yet. You will have to wear coins, of course, and we will create folds in your gowns so you can accept gifts. If you are asked to dance, it is customary that the man should give you an envelope of cash," blushed one of the younger wives.

"Unless he brings coins. Coins work!" one of the other wives said.

There was general agreement between the women. Shannon understood that perhaps the gold was more preferable. She wondered if the wives even had an opportunity to spend any money they would receive. And if they did receive cash, how would they spend it?

At last, every sari was unfolded, wrapped around her, and examined next to her skin to find the most flattering colors and textures for her complexion. She chose colors she enjoyed wearing or that made her happy. She stooped to count them neatly folded on the right side of the bed and discovered that they had selected twenty-two.

"A very auspicious number, twenty-two," the older wife said. "It is a balanced number. It is private and intimate, a perfect pair, just like a honeymoon should be. Twenty-two is a very good choice, my dear. I can't wait to see you all dressed up, your makeup just so, and your hair scented with jasmine and lavender. We are going to have such a wonderful time, Shannon."

"I have a question for you and perhaps a request," Shannon stated.

"Yes? What is it?" responded wife number one.

"Well, there is my friend, Rebecca. And—"

"Not Marco's former wife. You don't mean *that* Rebecca, do you?" the older woman asked. Several of the others in the group gasped at the thought.

"Well, as a matter of fact, yes. She and I have become friends. I'm just finding her cooperation and help to be useful. And I think even though Marco doesn't trust her—"

"He is wise, Shannon. You should take heed."

"Yes, I'm being careful. But I would like to have you have a session with her. I would like her to be pampered as well. Can that be done? And I have friends coming, as is customary here in the States. We call them bridesmaids here, and it's very common for the entire wedding party to have their hair, nails, and their makeup done all together as a group, going somewhere to be styled and made up for the wedding. Would it be possible I could have my friends, my bridesmaids as well? Or is that asking too much?"

The older woman's eyes grew wide. Her lips formed a straight line, and Shannon wasn't sure if there was disapproval or just confusion.

"Anything you ask of us, we will do, if we can. I am delighted to say that your girlfriends, your bridesmaids as you call them, would be most welcome. But Shannon, I am afraid I cannot bring Rebecca into our harem. The sultan has told us that she is not to be invited to the wedding. I hope you haven't asked her."

"I did, sort of. So I guess I'll have to fix that," Shannon said.

She felt awful and didn't approve of the opinion of Rebecca, but she understood where the sultan was coming from, and her attempt to ruin Marco's financial status was something she would not be forgiven by

Marco or any of the staff at the office. But Rebecca was proving to be useful and was working hard to try to get back into everyone's good graces. She was trying.

"This is not a debate, Shannon. It is simply not possible. Don't even ask, because even if Marco asked, the sultan would never allow it. He has to be careful who he invites to the island, and everybody will have to be vetted. I'm sure Marco is going to help with that process. But no matter how long it takes, Rebecca will never be allowed."

The reveal didn't sit very well in Shannon's stomach, but after all, the generosity of the sultan and his palace was so overwhelming, it softened the disappointment of not being able to include Rebecca. There was no way she could do anything but agree with them.

ALL AFTERNOON, THE women poured over other details of the many receptions and parties that were going to be hosted. There were certain of the wives who had daughters who would help with preparing the food, as well as taking care of guests, especially the children, on the guest list.

Shannon was shown pictures of some of the dishes they were going to be serving, foods she could never recall eating before even during her previous stay at the palace. It was explained to her also that she and Marco would not be spending their wedding night in the palace itself.

"There is a small cottage nestled in some man-groves and huge palm trees. It's a beautiful spot, and it has an unobstructed view of the bright turquoise ocean and pink sand." The young wife showed her a picture of a huge house, certainly not a cottage, of modern style with a metal roof adorned with cupolas and statues of various deities mounted in the eaves. All around the property was a bright green manicured lawn almost looking like it had been cut with scissors instead of a mower. Flowers bloomed, trees were trimmed, and benches and walks were available for walking at night by torch.

"You will love it there, and we only use the wedding house for newly married couples. No one lives there as a rule. It's very special, and it has lots of spirit."

"This doesn't look like a cottage. It must be three thousand square feet at least," Shannon said.

"I don't know," the older wife shrugged. "It's quite spacious inside with lots of light. With the jungle and the lush foliage and trees all around, it's like living in the middle of an exotic jungle. We are bringing pink doves and coral-colored parrots to release at the reception. I'm sure a few will manage to escape over to your side of the island. But other than those, you won't be intruded upon at all. It will be your own private paradise. Your meals will be provided. You can choose when they come and what you wish to eat."

"What if I want to cook?"

The group whispered amongst themselves in hushed tones. "My dear, your job is to please your husband. If you please him with your cooking, then yes, you may." Her eyes sparkled as she smiled.

In the background. Several of the other wives giggled, covering their mouths.

Shannon was fascinated with the culture that was going to be wrapped around her regardless of how she felt about it. She decided she was going to enjoy this time, because she knew that nothing like this wedding, the reception, the feast, or the parties would ever occur in her lifetime again.

As she glanced again at the boxes with their lids loosely reset, at the pictures, and the colors of decorations, flowers, the birds, and the grounds, she felt like she was living in the middle of a fairy tale. She was excited that this event, the start of her new married life, joined by the man of her dreams, her prince charming, would be remembered and talked about for years.

Her heart was filled with love and gratitude for the new family she'd acquired with the sultan and his wives.

She was the luckiest woman in the whole world.

CHAPTER 3

I WAS EXCITED to call our working group meeting, assembling the whole team in charge of the Trident Towers. After my meeting with the sultan, I had some fantastic news to share with everyone, and I had a feeling it was going to be extremely popular.

I took my time, examined the faces of my hand-picked staff, and finally landed with a smile that was warmly returned from my beloved fiancé, Shannon. Everyone was sitting in rapt attention, waiting for me to announce the good news.

"Today is a very special day for all of us, not just for me but for all of us. I have worked on the Trident Towers project for the past five years, eventually bringing this project to the attention of the public where we've received great support, in spite of the threats and the bombing of our office building earlier this year. The community has really embraced us, and it appears that most of, if not all, the obstacles that were in our way have been removed. We are green-light, full speed ahead, mates!"

The cheering went on for nearly a full minute before I could break in and add the rest of my news.

"Let me also tell you, in addition to the fact that we are moving full tilt on this project, that I have received the backing of one very important person."

I turned behind me and out from my office stepped the Sultan of Bonin. I had forgotten how small he was, and in his illness and present condition, which he hid very well, he looked even smaller and more shriveled. But his smile was wide, almost looking embarrassed as he bowed in greeting. Both his sons, who were seated at the long project table, stood out of respect for their father, but also for their sultan. The room clapped to welcome the sultan.

"So here's what we're going to do. The sultan and I have discussed his project in West Africa, and we both have come to the conclusion that now is probably not the best time to build there. It is an unsettled area, and it's getting worse by the month, with no clear dominant presence and no stable government to negotiate with for our protection and safety. We had a close call with Karin and our pilots and crew, a little too close for me. I'm not willing to jump right back in there again."

Karin looked down on her folded hands, a worried frown seizing the lower part of her face. I suspected that perhaps the remembrance of what she'd had to go through haunted her—being yanked off the plane and held hostage, all the money she brought for setting up the pre-construction phase of the project, paying for permissions and bribes, and not knowing if she would ever be able to return home in one piece. I considered that perhaps I wasn't being fair to her.

"Karin, we've made this shift, partly because of the sacrifice you made on that trip two months ago. I know how close it was, and we thought we were prepared, but we were blindsided. I would not forgive myself if I allowed anything like that to happen again, and since I'm also responsible for Khalil and Absalom, the sultan's two sons, I can't afford to fail. So, after a long discussion with the sultan, he has finally agreed instead to back our Trident Towers, which means that Khalil and Absalom will become co-project managers, overseen by Dax and the rest of our crew."

The group around the table clapped. Karin did not. But she bravely looked up to me and spoke. "I really did think I'd bought it that time, Marco. When you must face death like that, or the possibility of being held captive or prisoner for years, it changes you. I was prepared to tell you if you were going to be building in Nigeria that I was going to have to separate from the company."

The audience, several of the members who sat close

to her, touched her shoulders or patted her hands. Karin was a highly skilled negotiator, fluent in several African languages, as well as Chinese and Russian, and had been a fearless standard bearer of our company. But I could see that her close encounter was life altering. I was delighted I wasn't going to have to ask her to do that again.

"We all understand your sacrifice, Karin. It could have been any one of us in that same situation. And that's why this makes so much more sense. We will not have to take out a bank loan, which will reduce our costs, since the sultan has been very generous with us on the terms. His boys will be trained. They'll learn a great deal about building projects and how we do things here, as well as become familiar with the disabled population, particularly the community of wounded Navy SEALs. We're going to use them as much as possible so that they can help sell the project to others. I want the brothers to understand why it's important that we provide housing for these wounded heroes, and I know all of us will feel a great sense of pride when the project is finally done."

I stared at Karin until she returned my gaze again.

"In many ways, Karin, this is for you." I began to clap out of respect for the woman who almost gave her life for the chance to represent my company in an unstable environment. I'd known it was risky as hell, but yet I didn't follow my gut instinct, that knot in my stomach I should have paid attention to. I told her and the group that it was my miscalculation that caused their near-fatal capture.

"I feel I owe you an apology, but what I really want to say, Karin, is that I am filled with gratitude, and I'm honored to be able to work alongside you."

"Here, here," said Paul Vijay. "To the toughest broad I know, unstoppable, unsinkable, who refused to give up even against all the odds. You are the example of dedication and resolve, just like you are too, Marco."

The crowd clapped again. I noticed Shannon's eyes were filled with tears. I could see the sense of pride residing there, and I hoped that during our hopefully long married life, she would always look at me the way she was today. I drank in the admiration beaming from her beautiful face.

Several others made comments. Somebody asked the sultan when he might return to Nigeria. I knew the answer to that but couldn't reveal it.

"Well," he began, "that's a long painful subject, and I'm not sure it's worth the money and risk involved. Like Marco, I would feel very responsible if something happened to one of you. And since Marco is the expert, and he flatly could not guarantee my sons' safety, I really was in a way relieved. I had promised, and I wanted to keep that promise. But Marco showed me how we could still be a force for good, just not have to risk so much to do it."

The room agreed with his comments and let him know.

"I took the sultan over to the VA hospital in Tampa. He was much impressed with the orthotics lab there. I've arranged to hire a retired former Navy Lieutenant, Sam Connors, who lost both legs and an arm—"

"And an ear, don't forget the ear," the sultan interrupted.

"Yes, and an ear. I've hired him as a consultant on ADA requirements and to help be the liaison for some of the family members of disabled warriors we'll be working with. We're going to be customizing these homes so that they are retrofitted for whatever they need. For some, they may need altered cabinets and countertop heights, ramps, wide doorways for wheelchair access, elevators, and special appliances that can be operated with limited use of arms or legs. We want to make this experience as close to a normal living situation as is possible. It's our way of saying thank you to these men and women. And in honoring them, we become better human beings ourselves."

The new scope of the project was well received, and Shannon and Dax quickly removed themselves to the kitchen and brought out several bottles of champagne that we uncorked and passed around in small paper cups.

"To taking care of people who have lost everything but their hope and their will to live," said the sultan as he raised his glass.

It was worth drinking to, even if the cups were paper.

"YOU DIDN'T BREATHE a word of this, Marco. You kept me completely in the dark."

Shannon's arms were crossed at her chest. We were driving back to the construction site for our new home on the Gulf. I could tell from the corner of my eye she was stifling a grin.

"I have to have some secrets, don't I?"

"No, I don't think so," she said.

"I thought you like strong men who are mysterious, who do honorable things, but don't talk a lot about them."

"Oh, it's true, Marco. I hate salesmen. You don't have to sell me on you being a hero. I can tell there are some times you'd like to brag, but you don't do that."

"That's because I've seen a lot of the dark side of it. Going after evil is all-consuming sometimes. I'm not sure it's always heroic, but it is necessary. And the fact is, people like me, we're created to do that. I also knew you would like this change of venue."

"Oh, how so?"

"Shannon, don't play with me." I gave her a mock frown. "Would you rather that I head off to Africa and try to pick up where Karin left off, invest another two or three million, and possibly risk my life and not get back in time for the wedding? You honestly think I would do that?"

I could see her smile, her little mouth puckering at the edges. So sexy and so utterly kissable. I was about ready to pull the car over to the side and just ravish the heck out of her. But I decided to wait till later this evening instead.

"I think it's a wonderful idea, Marco. And I'm glad you were able to talk him out of the project in Africa. Florida is going to be a great place for the boys to learn their trade. And I have a feeling based on the past few days I spent with his wives that they were going to want to come over and inspect the process as well. They're going to miss Florida, Marco. I'm certain of it."

"I wouldn't mind entertaining the sultan and his group again. They can come as often as they like. But I'm just not sure how much time he has left. I think this is also a better solution for him. God forbid something happen to one of the boys. He'd have to spend his final days mourning instead of being able to reflect on a life well lived and a job, a worthy job, well done."

With her seatbelt still attached, she turned toward me, bringing her knees up onto the leather seat, leaned over, and kissed me. With her fingers, she rubbed the sides of my right temple, traced a finger lazily back and forth against my lower lip, and gave me a pre-dinner hard-on I knew I was going to have to take care of. That meant we'd be late for dinner, but oh my God, it would be so worth it.

It had been a good day. It was time to start celebrating.

And I was in the mood for some love.

CHAPTER 4

ALMOST A MONTH had passed since the sultan and his entourage returned to India, and Shannon corresponded with several of his wives through Harry. He'd procured a computer in secret and showed them how to find all the tutorials he wanted them to follow and how to navigate the web.

There were dozens of decisions that had to be made about the reception and the guest list, questions about seating and making sure we anticipated any problem that could pop up during the several days' events. Marco insisted that security be beefed up, so he sent over some of his best men, as well as a few new hires of recent retirees from the ranks of the Special Forces. He hired the best marksmen, men who were born protectors with years of experience navigating the dangerous arenas of the world.

So it was alarming when, with a little more than thirty days until the actual wedding event was to occur,

Marco got the call telling him the sultan had taken ill and was bedridden—possibly would remain bedridden for good. He decided, once he consulted with the sultan's doctors and Harry, as well as his wife number one, that a special hematologist would be flown over to help diagnose what was happening, monitor him, and guide the sultan back to some semblance of health, or at least help make him comfortable so he could conduct his affairs, tie up loose ends, and have a relatively pain-free existence. There was no question that his body was shutting down. No one was hiding the fact any longer. The sultan was gravely ill. It was hard to miss.

When the entourage had left in early November, Shannon had cried as she hugged all of the wives one by one and thanked the servants, the cooks, the dressers, and the dancers. The large boxes of saris were loaded, along with all the other luggage and trunks of new clothes they'd accumulated. They had taken private transportation hired by Marco's company.

It'd taken Shannon several days to get over the fact that these women, who had become like sisters to her, were halfway across the world and not accessible anymore.

So on this morning, Shannon and Marco both got up at dawn and made their way to the private airport at Tampa, took their hop to New York City for a refueling, and then flew directly to Mumbai, where they would travel the rest of the way by helicopter or water taxi. Shannon was instructed to pack lightly, since they were planning to stay only a few days. The hematologist they brought had a very busy, high-demand practice in Tampa and would not be available longer than a week. But he did agree to give Marco and the sultan that week.

Shannon loved flying on private planes. She loved the freedom of walking into the private jet terminal, waiting while the jet was fueled and inspected for flight, avoiding all the traffic of the normal airport milieu. But the best thing about flying private on his jet was that the food was wonderful and the bed in the back was extremely comfortable. She didn't have to sit strapped into a seat the whole time. She could rest, sip gourmet wines, even take a bubble bath if she so desired, and have a leisurely, stress-free trip.

Dr. Tramel had brought one of his medical student trainees and an expert nurse who had spent twenty years in the Army doing battle surgeries in field hospitals all over the globe. She was in high demand, especially in the specialized emergency rooms in the Tampa area.

But she preferred to work for Dr. Tramel. This crack medical team was legendary.

Dr. Tramel was reviewing the sultan's records,

making comments to the other two professionals, pointing out several things he wanted them to check out and consider, watch for. That gave Marco and Shannon time to slip to the back for a little bit of privacy and, if lucky, perhaps a lovemaking session.

The bedroom had been redecorated in calming shades of blue and green. The mattress was replaced with a foam pad that was so comfortable she nearly fell asleep just lying on the bed.

"Miss Marr, soon to be Mrs. Gambini, can I interest you in some whiskey perhaps?" Marco asked, holding up his bottle of Uncle Nearest.

"Of course. Are you trying to get me drunk?"

"Just warmed up a bit. Not that you need it. But I thought we could enjoy a little bit of private time over whiskey. What do you think?" he answered, giving her a kiss.

"I'm game."

As she sipped on the amber liquid in the small tumbler with one large ice cube circling the bottom, she thought about how much her life had changed since those days long ago when she was twelve years old and her older sister was alive. Marco was the shining prince, her fiancé. She thought about Emily and all that she'd missed out on, her death in the auto accident tragically taking everything from her. All their lives had changed overnight. Everything was different, forever altered by Em's death. Shannon felt like she was completing a circle of some kind, that she was finishing the job that had been started so long ago, that the love Emily had for this man was also the love Shannon shared with him as well.

It was nothing short of a miracle.

Marco set his glass on the bedside table and attended to the front of her blouse, unbuttoning each little pearl button carefully, almost delicately. His strong hands were scarred, and as he reached inside to touch the soft tissues of her chest, she felt the calluses on his palms and fingers, felt the results of his war years and the years thereafter, the scars that altered his flesh forever. As he touched her tenderly, she shivered with pleasure, ripples sparking down her spine, traveling along the backside of her thighs and then all the way down to her toes.

She needed him so badly.

Being the object of Marco's desire was an incredible experience for her every time they made love. This strong man knew how to be relentless and yet very tender and caring. His strong muscles and conditioned body held hers until she shattered, was totally spent, falling back to the mattress, covered in the sweat of their lovemaking. She was exhausted but still needed more. And it seemed like the more they were together, the more she couldn't be without him. The addiction for him was growing stronger. She wondered if something were to happen to him, would she lose the will to live?

Pushing those negative thoughts from her head, she set her sights on entering this doorway of her new married life. The team would do everything it could to repair the sultan's health. She'd finish making those last plans with the women of his household and then prepare herself to walk boldly into the rest of her future without regret.

She knew her life would be forever changed by the ceremony, her hand in his, the exchanging of rings, the commitment they would make to each other in front of everybody who was dear to them. She was ready to fully embrace this and the magic that came with it.

The shower they took afterward spurred another lovemaking session. She indulged in the scents of lavender and lemons, feeling the strength of his fingers shampooing her hair and covering her whole body with wet kisses.

Rubbing her head with a towel afterwards and wrapped in his big blue terry cloth robe with nothing on underneath, she had dangerous thoughts, perhaps trying to entice him a third time, and he very nicely kissed her neck and urged her to wait just a bit longer until they landed in New York. Reluctantly, she agreed.

Like everything else Marco asked her to do, she

found it impossible to refuse him.

They joined the rest of their party just twenty minutes before they began their descent into New York. If the doctor and his assistants suspected anything was going on in the back bedroom, they didn't let on. But Shannon still had a hard time looking them in the eyes without blushing.

On the ground for barely a half an hour, several catered meals were brought on board. The jet was prepared for takeoff, and shortly thereafter, they were in the sky again. They traveled with the sun to their backs until the dark night sky was pierced with twinkling lights and partially obscured by gray wispy clouds. The droning of the engines and Shannon's earlier exertions sent her into a deep sleep. She awoke just as they landed. Mumbai at sunrise sparkled like a golden jewel in the middle of the blue Indian Ocean.

They caught their limo driver, who also helped with the equipment Dr. Tramel brought as well as their luggage. He dropped them off at the water taxi port.

From there, they crossed the very still Indian Ocean. Shannon had never seen it so smooth and glassy before. It was as if they were sailing across an arctic lake, on a new adventure of some kind, to an undiscovered country or province. With the sun in their faces, they confronted the expectations of a dying man. Shannon braced for what she hoped would not be a sad encounter with him.

She had hope.

Shannon could tell just by the way Marco's distracted behavior manifested itself, Marco was concerned about the same thing.

As the Pink Palace and the coral pink sands of his island kingdom came into view, she was suddenly excited for the big day coming up in January, when she would become Mrs. Marco Gambini.

But first, there was work to do. She needed to be with an old friend and help his family begin the process of grieving.

CHAPTER 5

I KNEW THE instant our water taxi tied off that something was wrong. It was often something I felt on missions when I was a SEAL, just something in the air. It might be the certain call of a bird, the lack of noise, or a certain pungent smell, as if something evil or dangerous lurked in the bushes.

With the security detail I knew the sultan had, I doubted that could be a possibility. My men, and they were ten of my best, were spread out all along the island both on the shore and on the interior.

Shannon knew we were going to honeymoon in the new house the sultan had built on the opposite side, the north side. But I neglected to tell her we would be watched constantly. I knew she wouldn't like it, but I was hoping their skills would keep them from being discovered. Her life was far more important than her acceptance of some of my decisions.

My body was stiff, and the hair at the back of my

neck stood out, scratching against my polo shirt. It was like I had some preternatural remnants of an early warning system hardwired into my body from millions of years of evolution. Some would call it the remnants of early man's lizard brain. Many of my SEAL buddies claimed to feel the same thing.

It did interfere with us going on with our regular lives, since we saw danger everywhere we looked. We had to. It kept us alive.

Shannon was babbling on about something she'd been discussing with the nurse accompanying our hematologist. Two of the sultan's men took our luggage, and we boarded the small six-passenger golf cart while the luggage came behind in the small pickup. Along the peach-colored path of shells and sand, used as trails leading us to the palace, I searched the sky for evidence of a drone or sniper hiding in one of the tall palms, even a lookout hive that perhaps I wasn't aware of. I saw no evidence of cameras, lights, drones, satellites, or safe stations anywhere. But I still wasn't relieved.

There was something wrong, and I wasn't going to rest until I discovered what it was.

"Are you okay, Marco?" Shannon asked me. The sultan's driver moved our cart at a good clip, as it bounced and hummed taking small divots and crushing rocks beneath its tiny tires. The doctor and his two associates whispered amongst themselves from the third seat.

Shannon and I sat behind the driver, and my laptop was on the bench seat between us.

I looked over at her and realized I'd never answered her question, and she was not going to give up. She wanted an answer, and she would wait until I gave her one. I thought over the choices and decided, damn, I had to come clean. There was no way in the world I was going to have a better chance than now to explain how I felt.

I reached over and grabbed her hand, placing it on top of my thigh. I pressed both my palms against it. Leaning in toward her ear, I first kissed her earlobe and then whispered, "I'm just feeling something, and it doesn't feel right. I will figure it out, and then I'll let you know."

"Like what?" she said loudly, her voice carrying over the hum of the engine.

The doctor and his two assistants turned to study us.

I rolled my eyes and whispered in her ear again, "Please, Shannon, this needs to be quiet. I don't want you to draw attention to it. I promise I will let you know once I find out."

Shannon was quiet the rest of the trip to the palace.

There was a major construction project going on in

the front entrance, a large waterfall made with statues in coral and black granite, depicting beautiful naked women underwater, swimming, bathing, in various erotic poses that I feared some of Shannon's relatives wouldn't approve of. My team would love it, but Shannon's family could be easily offended.

The doctor whistled and scratched his beard. "Man, oh man, are you sure you're not taking me to a bordello, Marco?"

"You've seen the records, Doc. You've seen his pictures and his tests, and you know he has a harem of... I think it's still twelve or thirteen. Plus, he has a special someone in Brooklyn as well. Someone he never married. The man has appetites maybe you and I would fantasize about, but it seems to serve him well."

I could see the doctor wasn't buying any of it.

"He says he doesn't take any pills for performance enhancement, but somehow, I don't believe him. Do you know for sure?"

"Haven't got a clue. I doubt it, honestly. I mean why take a pill when you've got all these lovely ladies who can perform unspeakable acts of erotic fantasy—lovemaking and passion. He lives for those sessions, I know. I don't think the sultan would be capable of holding down a job ever. He likes women. It's his hobby, his passion, and I say, what the Hell. If you can afford it, then why not?"

The doc shook his head, skepticism making his jawline tense. His lips rolled down, and big worry lines developed at the bridge of his nose and on his forehead. He cocked his head at an angle and flicked his tongue, making a little ticking sound that was irritating as Hell.

"I've never quite run across a patient like him. In some ways, he's extremely well-preserved. He has a very strong heart, and his lungs are strong, although he's been developing some fluid, which is what happens with this form of cancer. Without much exercise, either. God, he must have a good diet is all I can say. All his other vitals are pretty darn normal. You'd think a man of his size, the opulence, and the way he lived would have Type II diabetes. On that score, he's healthy as a horse."

I found that funny.

"You're forgetting that he may not take walks or ride a treadmill or bicycle, but I'm willing to bet you he has sex perhaps three or four times a day, and I've heard through flimsy walls things I shouldn't have. I think he's got me beat."

We both laughed this time, the doctor placing his hand on my right shoulder.

Shannon trailed behind, and since I was carrying her heavy bag, she was carrying my briefcase containing my computer and sat phone.

The doors opened, and instead of my rotund friend, the sultan, we were greeted by a trio of younger wives, their eyes red and faces sad. I saw the house staff standing to the side, obviously pushed away so the women could greet me themselves, which was the custom for honored guests. It was remarkable that even in the face of such tragedy they still subscribed to some of these ancient rules.

Looking at the three women, all my fears were confirmed.

"So where is he? I presume he's in the bedroom?"

Like the three monkeys sitting in a tree, they all nodded quickly. The silver and gold jewelry jingled. They wore bangles on their ankles, bells on their wrists, and bright-colored saris that left a wide muscled midriff exposed. They were dressed for highbrow company, and it was important for the family to show their respect.

"I have brought the doctor, and we would like to examine him now if we could."

"Ah, Marco, I am so glad you have arrived!" It was Harry's voice I heard next, which completely shocked me.

"Harry? I didn't realize you were coming. Is—"

"No. The answer to your question, which I do not want you to ask, is no."

That's when I knew the beautiful Salima, his mother, wasn't coming or had not yet arrived. Harry was the lovechild of the sultan and the beautiful Salima. I figured she was back in Brooklyn, where the sultan had purchased them a brownstone.

Harry spoke up next. "Come this way. He's most anxious to see you. Maybe you can talk some of these women into leaving the room. Honestly, there are so many little noises and squeals and rattling of coins and bells and chains I don't see how he could sleep. And he needs his rest."

"Harry, I didn't introduce you to the doctor. Dr. Tramel, this is Harry, the sultan's private secretary." I winked after I said that, and Dr. Tramel appeared to recall the little story I'd told him about how the family didn't formally recognize Harry's paternity. It was going to have to stay that way.

After the two men chatted and Harry was introduced to the doctor's assistants, we were led into the huge chamber with the round bed atop a three-stepped dais strewn with exquisite throw carpets, barely covering some of the beautiful light pink and veined granite marble in the floor. The huge bed dwarfed the sultan as he lay in a relatively plain cotton nightshirt, although adorned with pearlescent stitching and tiny shell buttons. He was dozing in and out of consciousness and didn't seem to recognize we had entered the room.

"May I?" Dr. Tramel asked Harry.

Harry deferred to the sultan's first wife, who stood, released the sultan's hand from her grip, bowed, and stepped backwards to allow the doctor to examine her husband.

I moved to the other side of the bed, holding Shannon's hand, our fingers laced tightly together. I felt the large green, emerald ring that I'd given her recently. Her delicate floral scent was the right kind of intoxicating to me. I also detected the faint scent of our lavender shower gel from the plane.

It brought a smile to my face.

She leaned her head against my shoulder and watched as the doctor pulled the gown from the front of his chest, opened it carefully, listened to his heart, examined his eyes, and checked the tips of his fingers and his fingernails. Then he pulled aside the covers to examine his feet. Both ankles were extremely swollen to the point that, if the sultan were to stand, the flesh would roll over his ankles. His toes were stuck in a reflexive strained, pointed position that looked painful. Occasionally, his legs jerked.

The skin at the back of his heels was separated, cracking and infected, showing an angry shade of red. These issues with his legs and toes hadn't appeared when we were in Florida. Perhaps walking on the beach and the saltwater had healed him in some respect. But here, it looked to me like he was getting very weak and might not be well enough to even sit up or walk.

Dr. Tramel came over to me quietly and, as he put his arm around Harry's shoulders, whispered to the two of us, "I'm not sure exactly what is going on, but it appears he is fighting some kind of an internal infection. He also has involuntary muscle spasms. And that's not the cancer. There's something else going on. It's almost like an allergic reaction that's taken hold of his body. His heartbeat is strong, but his pulse is faster than I'd like it to be. I don't see where he's ever been on blood pressure medication so perhaps that could help. I'd also like to put him on a water pill for those ankles but want to see a blood test first. At the least, he's going to have to have some treatment because leaving those ankles and toes and nails as they are will lead to further infection, and he risks amputation. Somehow blood is not getting to his extremities. His fingers, the tips of them are blue if you notice."

"Doc, does he appear dehydrated?" Harry asked. "Because he's been drinking lots of water. He seems to want water more than anything else. The water seems to stop the spasms slightly."

"Well, I have some ideas about that, but this doesn't look like a long-term reaction to any of his cancer medications or his long-term treatment. This is something else. And it almost feels like some foreign substance he's been exposed to."

The question that immediately rose in my mind was if he'd been poisoned, and I whispered such to the doctor.

"Yes, Marco, I think you could be right. It's not arsenic. His breath doesn't have that almond smell. But somehow, he's leaching out nutrients from his body, and maybe the thirst is coming from that. His body is trying to heal itself, but these spasms are worrisome. I'm going to have to run some tests. I researched and found a lab in Mumbai that will do things on a twenty-four-hour turnaround, unless the tests take longer. It's expensive, but they will send a helicopter to pick up any lab work that I have and promised I could have the results within hours. I think I better start by taking some labs, maybe a urine sample if we can get it, and then we'll have to go from there."

He looked at the sultan's number one wife, who had been conversing with a small cluster of wives in the corner. She approached, apprehension showing in her face.

"You have news for me? Please tell me it's good news."

"Ma'am, you know he has a chronic condition from which he will not survive. But this sudden turn is caused by something else. I want you to limit and insist on it—" He looked at me and then back to the woman.

"I want only certain people to handle him. We'll need to bathe him."

"Oh, we can do that, that's our job."

"Okay, as long as everybody bathes before and after they handle him. I can't be sure that he hasn't picked up some kind of toxin in his system. It might be transmitted if you aren't careful."

"Yes, we will do that. We will take shifts. And when they bring in the food, we will feed him. We won't let anybody else feed him," she said as she shook her head, dangling her hoop earrings and making the bells around her neck chatter.

"Listen, it's not only who gets to feed him, I want to make sure his food's being prepared properly. I would feel a whole lot better, Marco, if we could bring in somebody else from the outside to prepare his meals. With the swelling and the deterioration of his circulation, I'm feeling like there's something that he's ingested internally. But I won't know for sure until we do the blood tests."

"That can be arranged," I said.

"We can do that," his wife added. "We want to take care of him, and he has daughters who can help in the kitchen. We don't need to bring anybody else from the outside. We can use the kitchen staff to help prepare things we're going to need for the wedding."

Shannon squeezed my hand at the mention of the

wedding. That got me to chuckle. "Oh, so it's okay if they poison us and the guests at our wedding, but it's not okay for them to serve the sultan, is that what you're saying?"

"Not at all, Marco. There is much to do to prepare. We will be his servants, his cooks. We will bathe him, protect him from the outside world. Frankly, I wouldn't feel right if he passed away under any other circumstance. I would feel horribly guilty. We need to take care of him. It's our mission. Centuries ago, if he were to die, we would all die with him. In a way, not much has changed. Our loyalty to our sultan is a primary concern. Even the children and grandchildren feel the same way."

The doctor had begun the process of drawing blood, and even that didn't rouse the sultan from his fitful sleep. Dr. Tramel's emergency nurse was on the satellite phone, probably to the lab in Mumbai arranging the lab work pickup. I slipped out of the bedroom and into the hallway, examining who was watching the sultan's door. I was surprised that there were no guards posted at his bedroom door, which is what I had asked. This was just one more thing that didn't make sense to me. Had these people disobeyed me? Or was there some change of plans?

Shannon walked up behind me and placed her arms around my waist, pressing her forehead into my back between my shoulder blades.

"Oh God, Marco, I hate seeing him like that. I'm hoping, whatever is going on, that he can recover. I don't want to put these people through a wedding when he's so sick. Do you think we should make other arrangements?"

I turned around, matching her arms around my waist by doing the same to hers. I tipped her chin up and gave her a gentle kiss, whispering, "The invitations have all been sent out. The wedding is here. He would be furious if we canceled it. It has nothing to do with whether it's easy. It is what one good friend does for another to honor the doorway we are to walk through. This isn't just a celebration. It's a mark in time, a mark in history, a point from which we go forward."

She melted into my arms, leaning against my chest, mumbling her agreement and understanding.

To the top of her head, I added, "We'll sort it out, Shannon. Let's not worry yet. We have lots of things to do while we're here, and if someone has done something despicable, I promise you, they will pay for it with their life."

CHAPTER 6

T HE FOLLOWING MORNING, Shannon and the entire team were relieved the sultan appeared to be improving. They awaited the results of testing that had been ordered and flown to Mumbai for analysis. The sultan was still delirious, wild-eyed, and occasionally had fits of agitation and muscle tenseness. It made sense to Shannon that he had been exposed to something rather than this being the result of his cancer treatments or something related to his other illnesses.

Marco approached her tenderly, taking her in his arms.

"Why don't you go with a couple of the wives and take a tour of the cottage, maybe go explore the rest of the island? I'll send one of my guys with you."

Marco had used his fingers to put quote marks around the word *cottage*. It really wasn't a cottage at all but a massive, contemporary glass and steel architecturally-designed home with stunning views of the blue

Indian Ocean.

It was a tempting offer.

"We still don't have the results, and I know that his family is going to want to know as soon as possible. I am heartened that he's better, but he's still not out of the woods, Marco. I think I better stay."

"Well, then if we get some news, I think you should wander a bit, just have them entertain you. I'm going to need some serious discussions with the sultan once he's more coherent. And if he is not getting significantly better or if this is the result of something else more serious, then of course I'm going to ask the boys to fly over as well."

"I think that's a good plan. The boys' mother doesn't want them to come over, worrying them unless it's absolutely necessary," she answered.

Shannon knew Marco was all about the planning, the contingency planning, and the backup planning. And until the immediate family and household could be eliminated from suspicion, he had some serious interviews to conduct.

He pressed his palm to her cheek. "I wish I could spend more time, but we knew this wasn't a vacation. I can't wait for our big day, and I'm hoping nothing will stop that from happening."

"Me too, Marco. And I understand. I think perhaps I'll take a nap, and then let's see what the day brings. I could just hang out in their quarters, but I've developed a little jet lag."

She smirked at him and then smiled.

"That's your fault, sir," she said as she pointed to his chest.

"Guilty as charged." His raspy, sexy voice tickled her insides deliciously.

"And I have a few office things I need to take care of. We've set up some interviews, and if I'm not going to be there, I'm going to ask Rebecca if she can fill in."

Marco growled. She was on delicate ground.

She'd decided yesterday to approach the subject of inviting Rebecca to the wedding.

"Marco, I wanted to talk to you about—"

"The answer's no, Shannon. She's not coming. I still don't trust her. If you think that the sultan or his family will accept her, you're extremely naïve. Be warned, if you push the subject, you're only going to alienate them. So please, Shannon, drop it. Figure out another way you and Rebecca can resume your friendship, but she is not going to attend this wedding, and I don't care if you promised it to her or not. She's not allowed on this island or anywhere close to this island, and she's not going to be a part of our ceremony. I really need you to understand that, Shannon."

With his hands on Shannon's shoulders, he stared directly down into her eyes. She could see that it was useless to try to argue with him and relented, for now.

"I won't make a scene. I promise. I got your message, and I will fully comply."

Marco wiggled his eyebrows at her last comment.

"Fully comply? Hmm... Just what did you have in mind?"

She pushed his chest with both her palms, throwing him off balance. But with one step backwards, he became a concrete wall again. She needed to change the subject.

"It's wonderful that you were able to convince him to do the project in Florida. It was a worry and a concern hanging over my head, and I knew it would hang over my head the entire pre-planning and the parties and the wedding itself. Even the honeymoon was going to be spoiled by the possibility you might have to leave to go to a part of the world where the odds were extremely high you and the rest of the team could be injured. So, thank you, Marco. Thank you for taking care of it in such a professional manner. I honestly think it was the best way this whole building project could have developed. And I'm going to work my damnedest to make sure we pull it off with all the bells and whistles and all the hopes and dreams you originally had for the project, and more."

He embraced her in his strong arms, kissing her neck, the side of her cheek, and her hairline. His soft lips began grazing across hers, setting her libido on fire. And then finally he planted a deep kiss on her lips, which turned her knees and toes to butter. She squeezed him tightly, moved her arms up around his neck, and whispered, "I love you so much, Marco. We have so much to look forward to."

Two hours later, with the sun well down toward the horizon, Shannon was awakened by noises coming from downstairs. The women were agitated, and there was arguing occurring in the great hall, stretching all the way down the hallway to the harem quarters. With the beautiful marble and travertine floors and the jewel encrusted inlaid columns in the grand ballroom they called their living room, the whole place echoed with worried and anxious voices. She knew something important had happened.

She slipped on her leather sandals and flew down the twisted stairwell to the ground floor, coming upon a group of several of the wives clustered in front of the doors to the sultan's bedroom.

She examined the faces of the women and sensed there was news about the sultan.

She asked one of the younger wives. "What's happened?"

"He is much better. The doctor has prescribed an anti-toxin and other things to help flush his system out. They have discovered from the tests that he has been poisoned. It's strychnine."

"Strychnine? How could he be poisoned with strychnine?"

"Apparently, very easily. I guess the house uses it for pest control. It grows wild here, all over India as well. The seeds, when ground into a fine powder or poultice, are very toxic.

"Is there a traitor in the house?" Shannon asked.

"Marco is interviewing several of the staff, especially the cooks."

"Will he recover fully?" Shannon asked.

One of the other wives inserted herself. "We're not exactly sure, but we are relieved to know the doctor says he will recover. As to recovering fully, that we have to wait and see."

The younger of the two wives looked terrified. She was being very brave but finally her nose puckered as her upper lip quivered, and then Shannon noticed the tears overflowing, spilling over her colorful cheeks, making streaks in her makeup. She collapsed in Shannon's arms.

Stroking the young wife's beautiful hair, Shannon whispered, "It's going to be fine. You'll see. He has the very best doctors, and they will figure out what needs to happen. You need to be strong for him, right?"

The young wife nodded her head with resignation

and left to gather a couple of children who had migrated to the hallway near the sultan's bedroom.

Shannon wanted to visit with the sultan, but she knew the doctors were probably with him and, in time, Marco would fill her in completely. One by one, the wives faded back into their private wing, and eventually, the sultan's number one wife exited the door, closing it softly behind her. She gave Shannon a brave smile.

"Have you heard?"

"One of your sisters told me it was poison. Are we suspecting anybody, anybody on the palace staff?"

"Marco is interviewing the kitchen help now. It definitely is something he ingested, and the doctor says he will not remember what made him sick. We are hoping there will be no lasting issues, in light of his already weakened state."

Her shoulders were stooped over, her shiny black hair wrapped in a tight bun shielded in a colorful headscarf tied at the back of her neck.

Shannon touched her hands. "You should go get some rest. I'm sure if there's any change they will come get you."

She nodded. "I am exhausted, I admit it. But that was wonderful news finding out that he can recover. I just hope we got it in time. First, I am going to see what kind of mess our kitchen is, and then I'm going to turn in early."

"Is he with the doctor, anyone else with him?" Shannon asked.

"Yes, just the three of them. We bathed him, as apparently that helps with the healing as he sweats out the poison. I have to bathe again and thoroughly clean these clothes or perhaps burn them."

She held out to the sides the colorful sari she was wearing, and Shannon regretted the fact that perhaps this beautiful item would have to be destroyed.

"So we don't know if others have been contaminated?"

"That's correct. There is a team coming from your Navy, I believe—a HAZMAT team. They're going to do a thorough sweep of the palace, the kitchen, the water supply. We have to bring in food and water for now because we have to find out where this came from first. But it's most likely ingested through his food or perhaps the water he drank, although strychnine is supposed to be a very bitter substance. The doctor thinks it was probably laced into some food prepared for him that would be rather spicy so he wouldn't notice. He loves his yellow curry and eats it almost every day. And so far none of the children or the wives or myself have any symptoms. I think he was targeted for some particular reason."

She rubbed her eyes and sighed again. "Why in

God's name would anyone want to harm him?"

Shannon whispered to the wife, "Perhaps it had to do with those men the boys were dealing with, with the drug smugglers with the stolen boat?"

"It's hard to say. It almost feels like it's personal, though, doesn't it?" she answered.

Shannon agreed. "You go check on the kitchen. I'm going to wait in the living room until somebody comes to get me. I don't want to be in anybody's way."

As the sultan's first wife wafted away amid sounds of silks and bangles, Shannon tried to make herself comfortable in the great hall. She brought out her cell phone, nestling herself in a red leather couch facing the fireplace. It seemed silly to have a fire in such a warm part of the world, but the fire and the spiced wood they burned was like incense, which soothed her nerves. She was grateful for it.

Dialing the office, she was put through to Dax so she could update everyone on their discovery.

"Jeez, Shannon, the hits just keep on coming, don't they?" Dax said.

"Well, that's true, and I suppose I will find out more later, but I just wanted to ease everybody's mind. It looks like he will pull through, although I haven't seen him, and I haven't been able to talk to Marco. But hearing from some of the sultan's family here, they seem to think he will make a full recovery."

"Thank God!."

"What kind of a weakened condition he will remain is yet to be seen. I'd like you to get hold of the boys and let them know. I don't want them to worry."

"Oh, you got it, Shannon. Hey, those guys have been working really hard. I wasn't sure at first it was going to be something I could tolerate. They've been raised so different, but every single task I have given them, they've willingly tackled. I have to remind them to ask questions, because they are so smart they want to figure it all out themselves. Sometimes, it's actually better if you ask questions so you can get it done right the first time, know what I mean?"

"Point taken. You keep bugging them until they learn."

"And they are learning. I like their attitude too. There's been a big shift, and I'm sure you've noticed it as well."

"I have. Is there any other news?" Shannon asked.

"Well, we've got some really good bids on the flooring, and I'm supposed to pick up the preliminary electrical and plumbing permits tomorrow morning. We already got the underground just before you left, but people are most anxious to get to work here, and we're getting lots of really good labor prices. Wish I could say the same for the materials, but that's a work in progress. I actually think we're going to come in under budget. I really do."

Shannon was pleased. "That's great news. Marco is going to love hearing that." She hesitated and then asked, "And Rebecca? How's she behaving?"

"I've not seen much of her, thank God. I'm not sure whether she really has a place in this organization. I admire you for trying, but without you here, Rebecca just seems to be hanging on to an old life she doesn't own any longer. She needs to find her own gig."

Shannon knew Dax was telling the truth. She had a keen sense of reading human nature, and Shannon had grown to respect that.

"So we're still a go for January then?"

"Yes, Dax, the wedding's still going forward as planned. Can't wait for you to see all their beautiful preparations here."

"So when do you think you guys will come back, or are you going to stay?"

"Oh no, we'll be back in a few days I'm sure. We've got way too much to do. The last thing I want is have to be checking in with the office while we're on our honeymoon. If I don't do the work before the wedding, that's what's going to happen, and you know it."

"Damn right about that. Well, I think we're in good shape. Did you meet the young Navy lieutenant, Sam?"

"Yes! Marco introduced me to him once. How's he working out?"

"He's a dynamo. I mean he has some really good friends that are very well connected in the community, not only with the SEALs but in the disabled community. There are lots of grants available and companies that might be willing to underwrite part of the project in exchange for promotional opportunities. Sam is looking into that for some of our costs. We had a large electrical contractor from Orlando approach us about donating their fees, their labor. That would be huge. That will probably save us if it comes through nearly three hundred thousand, Shannon."

"Fantastic, Dax. And Sam has done all this?"

"He has. He attended a dedication for a children's hospital in the Orlando area where this electrical contractor donated their services to that cause. It was for children of service members—police, fire, and first responders—who lost their lives in their line of duty, and the children's hospital specializes in cancer treatment and makes sure that the widow and children of the fallen warrior never have to pay a hospital bill again. This program that Marco started here with the Trident Towers, it's right up their alley. It's perfect for them."

"That's awesome. Well, as soon as I'm finished here, I can't wait to get back and finish work on my to-do list, which is steadily getting larger instead of smaller. I'm going to try to make contact with Rebecca now, but in case I don't, if she comes in, would you tell her I'm trying to reach her?"

"Will do, Boss. You take care, and give the big fella a hug and kiss from me, okay?"

"Absolutely. And I'll give one to the sultan too. Especially the sultan, from you."

The last thing Shannon heard as she disconnected the phone was Dax's laughter. It warmed Shannon's heart.

She sat in the great room, feeling like a princess in the kingdom of make-believe. She'd never imagined she'd someday get married on an exotic island, in a pink palace with a jewel-encrusted room, with Prince Charming himself at her side.

They had come so far, had endured so much in these months, it would have been horrible if everything they'd worked for evaporated in a puff of smoke, like waking up from a magical dream. Everyone looked to Marco as the leader of the project, the chief strategist, but Shannon began to realize the sultan was actually the glue that held everybody together.

He was their host for the wedding, he was their largest benefactor, and he was probably Marco's best friend at this point. Marco was one hundred percent dedicated to making sure the sultan was going to leave a legacy in the world.

Shannon loved her husband-to-be more and more

every day, because Marco's life was larger and more meaningful than Shannon had ever thought possible.

And the more she spent time with Marco, the better person she became as well.

Something slipped into her mind which made her smile. She thought of a phrase she could use to describe her life now.

She was going to call it Marco's magic.

CHAPTER 7

THE KITCHEN, PREP, and wait staff were lined up next to a wall leading to the courtyard garden at the side of the sultan's palace. They consisted mostly of men, but there were several women in the group of twelve. I could see they were terrified of the possibility they'd be interrogated or perhaps accused of being an accomplice to the poisoning.

"I just want to find out who's responsible for this and why, and I'm starting with the group of you here who are the kitchen staff and the wait staff, but I'm going to check everybody who could have had contact with the poison materials and the sultan. First of all, I'm going to call you in one by one and ask a series of questions. You have nothing to fear if you have no responsibility for any of this. But trust me, if you know anything or suspect anything and you don't inform me, it will go very badly for you. I am not here to dole out punishment or to beat you into giving a confession.

But I warn you, the sultan is going to survive this attack, and his methods may not be as kind as mine."

I paced in front of them, staring each person straight-on, hoping to put the fear of God in their souls.

"So look upon me as your last chance to avoid very unpleasant circumstances."

The staff sometimes looked amongst themselves and sometimes looked down at their hands or feet, but I didn't notice anybody who had an attitude that stood out from all the rest. Culturally, they came from many different countries in the Indian basin, even parts of Africa. I had their files. While some had been in the sultan's employ for generations, nearly considered family members, there were a handful who were fairly new hires. I was going to focus on those first, thinking it would likely be the best method of catching the probable culprit or culprits.

There was going to be no kitchen preparation today, and several trusted servants were dispatched to obtain food elsewhere off-island. As soon as the Navy team arrived, the entire kitchen would be searched—every crack in the tile countertops, behind stoves. In short, every square inch of the place would be thoroughly inspected and tested for the presence of strychnine. Later, we'd test the grounds and the residences of all the people living here. They were to take hair samples from families, even the pets would undergo testing.

I was told only two people were not present today who had worked this week for the sultan's family. We were in the process of retrieving them, but they were said to be off-island. That concerned me. But I knew we'd find them.

After the kitchen staff, I was going to interview the housekeeping staff, the groundskeepers, and some of the carpenters and workmen, although those individuals were typically second-, third-, or fourth-generation employees of the sultan's family and really would have nothing to gain from his demise. I suspected there was some personal motive, not a huge smuggling operation or political assassination attempt at work here, as the sultan had few enemies and he protected his kingdom well. I needed to find out the motive.

The head chef's office was vacated so I could conduct my interviews. Several of the staff members who were going to be interviewed first did not speak English. We chose—at the suggestion of the sultan's number one wife—one of his other wives who was most fluent in several languages, more than a dozen at least, to be our translator. She sat next to me behind the mahogany desk. I made sure the chair the interviewee was sitting on was two or three inches shorter than mine, was uncomfortable, and squeaked with the slightest movement.

The sister-wife introduced me, and I tried to repeat the man's name but of course butchered it. She smiled and proceeded to tell me what the background of the employee's family was. He was an older gentleman who appeared to be about the sultan's age.

"He is the brother of a childhood playmate of my sultan, Marco. Sadly, his brother was killed in a fishing accident several years before, and the family came into hard times. Sultan hired him about a year ago, as he was well-known in the southern ports of India for being an excellent cook for some of the big houses there."

"Thank you, that was very complete." I looked over the file that had his picture, writing I couldn't interpret, and a tiny scrawled signature almost resembling an X. Perhaps he was not someone who had attended school and could read or write.

"If you will translate for me, I'm going to ask him several questions. Please explain this to him."

She did as she was told, and the cook nodded in agreement. His eyes darted back and forth, and I could see his chest was shiny with beads of sweat.

As I spoke, she translated.

"Just as I said earlier, you have nothing to fear if you have nothing to hide. I'm going to ask you several times if you have observed anything or if you know anything about the poisoning of the sultan. Are you familiar with poisons?"

He spoke back to the wife, shaking his head.

"He says that, in his village, which was not the same village the sultan's friend was raised in, they were brothers but not raised together, several holy men knew how to make potions. He had no taste for any of that, and he felt, as a Hindu, he was commanded to be respectful of all peoples and all beings."

"Okay, so would you know what a poisonous plant or seeds would look like? Have you ever seen anything someone has told you is poisonous?"

The gentleman nodded his head yes.

"He says they have rats on the island, and there is bait for the black traps that are here. There also are snakes and other animals that get into the garbage. It is a problem on this island, but the bait and traps seem to keep it under control. He says he is not the one who prepares the traps."

"Ask him where the poison is for these traps."

"He says he does not know. He does know where some of the traps are placed, but he does not know who prepares them or where the poison is stored."

"Ask him who does know?"

"He says he believes it is the prep chef, the woman they know as Seema."

I searched the files and saw that Seema was indeed

someone I was going to be interviewing at the front of the line.

I continued. "Where has he worked in the past?"

As we kept up our translated dialogue, the man seemed to relax slightly, revealing more and more about his family, his past, and some of the incredible misfortunes that he had experienced as a young child and a young man. He showed his left foot, which was turned to the side, giving him a noticeable limp, a deformity he said from birth. He tried to work as kitchen staff several places before he landed several good jobs working for wealthy families. But one by one, as the family dynasties changed and financial situations were altered by events, he was either relieved of his duties or absorbed into another household where occasionally the owner would beat them.

"He found that as a disabled cook, he was often the brunt of everybody else's scorn."

I was not familiar with his culture, but there was something in the look of him, in his eyes, that I trusted. I decided that he was not going to benefit from killing the sultan, had no animosity, and actually had much to lose if he were to be terminated from this particular job. He had no wife or children to support, so living on the island in a modest house was probably the best he could ever hope for. There would be no reason he would want to disturb that.

We interviewed three others, all with similar stories, several recounting how the sultan had been kind to them when they were either sick in the hospital or had suffered a family tragedy. I began to see a pattern, which I should have guessed, but had never known before. The sultan liked to do things for people who'd not been as fortunate as he had. It was completely consistent with what I knew of the man himself.

When I interviewed Seema, she reflected the same nervousness initially that all the rest of the kitchen staff I'd interviewed displayed. She was difficult to open up, but when she did, she volunteered that she was aware the poison for the rat traps was something that would be harmful to pets and to humans. And she kept the poison in a special closet in her cottage, under lock and key. She said she had checked the closet after word got out that it was strychnine poising, and nothing appeared to be out of the ordinary.

"As far as she understood, no one else had a key to the storage closet."

"You can see how it looks for you, Seema. You can see that you have access to what may have poisoned him. We aren't sure, but you can see that. Have you ever seen any of that substance in the kitchen or outside of your home, or have you ever seen any of the traps missing or broken apart?"

That seemed to elicit a reaction. Her eyes lit up as

she recounted that several nights ago she went to replace the bait in several of the boxes and could not find one. It had been placed along the path they took to empty the garbage, the path where things were burned and not allowed to attract pests from the jungle. She didn't like to walk through the dense foliage because of snakes and other predators out there, so she didn't go search for it. And she didn't consider that there was anything out of the ordinary, so she didn't report it. But she took a new box out there and to the best of her knowledge, that box was still in place today.

It was a very lucky break, if in fact that turned out to be the source of the poison. But I still didn't have the motive. One thing that did relieve me, however, was that this was something that one person could do by themself. It wouldn't require a whole team, or a group of conspirators to pull off. And that made it even more likely my hunch was correct. This act was personal.

As I did with all the interviewees, I always ended the conversation by asking them who they would suspect. And like all the others, she shook her head, wished she could help, but said she had absolutely no inkling that someone would want to do him harm.

In between appointments, my security team informed me they had located both of the employees who were not here today but had been working during the time the sultan was poisoned. I was told they would be brought in tomorrow morning, early.

I finished the interviews late. Those who traveled by boat off the island at night were told to remain on the grounds, and a facility was provided for them. Those individuals were monitored and watched even more closely than the residents of the island. I received word that the Navy team was going to arrive first thing in the morning, near dawn. I made a list of all my questions and the places I wanted them to search first, gathered my notes together along with the files of the men and women of the staff, and asked for permission to begin interviewing the housekeeping staff in the morning.

Harry greeted me, handing me a longneck beer, which I was grateful for. I mockingly wiped the top of it off and examined it closely before I took a sip.

"Oh, so I see you're going to interview me too then, is that right, Marco?"

"I'm just messing with you, Harry. So how is your mom?"

"She's worried. She wants to come to your wedding, but I just—I don't know if that's going to be possible. She also wants to say goodbye. I'm hoping he will allow it."

"That would be nice, but politically, well, I've had no experience on that score since I'm only married to one woman at a time, but I certainly wouldn't want to be the one to straighten all that out. Does she have any friends among the wives?"

"I think the younger ones are more open-minded. But his number one wife will not be happy. She would put her foot down, and he would have to honor her request. I think if we are able to arrange it, if he's agreeable to it, it's going to have to be kept from her. I hate to do that, but I think that's the only way it'll happen. My mother may not want to press it. And maybe that would be the best."

I felt for Harry, living in one world, roots in another, robbed of a father, who nonetheless provided for him. He was lucky to have such a worldly and giving mother, who loved him absolutely to the ends of the earth. But Harry was, even though a US citizen, very connected to the sultan. He was proud of his heritage, and I could see his father's passing was going to be tough for him, perhaps even harder than it would be on his mother. For his mother had experienced the sultan's love, knew that she was his favorite even though he'd never married her. Harry never got to experience that. For his own safety, he was raised clear across to the other side of the globe in a Brooklyn brownstone.

I needed to get to bed, and after conferring with Dr. Tramel and getting his update, I was satisfied that the sultan was going to be up and walking tomorrow.

He advised me not to visit, since they'd finally gotten him to the point where his muscle cramping had stopped. I learned this was a symptom of strychnine poisoning, and often patients died not from the poisoning itself but from cardiac arrest because they could never rest their bodies. They were in constant motion until it just literally wore them out.

As prescribed, the sultan was drinking huge quantities of water, which was good, and the lab in Mumbai had delivered a portable testing kit so he could monitor the sultan's blood with a finger prick and test for the presence of the poison. Dr. Tramel told me that his count was coming down quickly. He thought there would be very little trace of it left within three days.

"Are you any closer to finding out who did this?" he asked.

"I'll see what the Navy boys say. But I think the easiest possibility would be a rodent bait set out by the garbage dump. The purpose is to kill rats and snakes that might come to feed off the garbage. I've identified who prepares the traps, and we've also verified that one of the kits is missing. So it could be a crime of opportunity. I'd be surprised if that wasn't the source."

"Good work, Marco. It doesn't take very much to kill a person, about a half cup. But I think what may have happened is the first dose didn't kill him, so it was given again and again, possibly for several days. The chemical is quite bitter, very difficult to disguise, so they would have to be careful not to get exposed. That said, it's just a guess. But I think we are dealing with an inexperienced person who found a way to do this, not someone who planned it long-term or was a trained assassin."

"Well, Doc, I'm bushed. And if I'm ever going to get married, I better get upstairs and see my lovely fiancée before she decides, 'Hey, maybe I'll go home with the doc instead.'"

We both had a good laugh at that.

I climbed the staircase, my eyes traveling over the great hall—the hallway down to the women's quarters, the area off to the right where the kitchen and the staff would normally be busily washing dishes and preparing food for the next day. I glanced at the torches lit in the hallway leading to the sultan's room and was satisfied there were two of my men outside his door, both armed and extremely lethal. The doctor had told me that his number one wife was spending the night with him in bed. Which was only allowed after they stripped and burned the sheets, changed his nightshirt, and bathed him. The doctor had told me he thought it was safe.

I had done all I could at this point, and I knew there would be a lot more to discover tomorrow when the team arrived. But we were getting closer.

I opened the door to the bedroom and instantly was transported to another world. She lay naked on the bed, her hands above her head, tied to the ornate bedframe with red silk sashes. She had lit candles all around the room, and I saw a chilled bottle of champagne next to the dresser. She'd probably waited there for me for a long time, because several of the candles had dripped onto the furniture and floor. She'd fallen asleep against her arm. I quietly closed the door and locked it. Without taking my eyes off of Shannon's beautiful body, I slowly stripped off my clothes, my hard-on swollen and almost painful. I very gently climbed onto the bed, placed my knees over her hips, leaned into her face, and kissed her.

Her body responded immediately as she moaned and began to writhe on the bed beneath me. "Are you all done, Marco?" she whispered, her lips calling me.

"No, sweetheart. I've only just begun."

CHAPTER 8

WHEN SHANNON AWOKE in the morning, Marco had already left to go meet with the Navy advance team. She arched up, stretching her arms to the headboard, fingering the red silk bonds he had lovingly tightened and then released during their hours-long lovemaking session. Her total exhaustion was delicious. She would miss him, knew he'd be busy all day today, and ached for him to return.

All in due time.

She knew she had to be patient.

She slipped on her clothes, enjoying the casual feel of her khaki pants and the leather flip-flops, then ran down the stairs to ask questions and seek information. Her belly was starved and gurgling.

She heard noises in the kitchen and smelled fresh coffee so made her way through the doorway and was greeted with several smiling faces. A mug of coffee with cream was placed in her hands. She greeted the staff, took a sip, and declared it excellent. Her thumbs-up was returned.

She was shown to a seat at the table where she was brought some eggs and some fruit. An overflowing bowl containing colorful fruits from all over the island had been placed in the middle of the long table that could easily feed thirty. Other than bananas and papayas, she didn't recognize anything.

One of the sultan's younger wives marched past to get some coffee herself.

"I've already had my sip, and these eggs are fantastic, so I guess the kitchen's been tested and it's clean?" she asked the wife.

"Yes, they were here nearly two hours ago, Shannon. They found no trace of the chemical. They're outside working on the grounds. I think they're going to do some of the other rooms and cottages later. Are you feeling well?"

"Yes." Shannon smiled, then blushed, and closed her eyes.

Her companion at the table giggled, placing her red painted fingernails over her mouth. "I see. I'm happy for you."

Shannon wondered if any of the women in the harem ever had boyfriends outside of the palace. She had never considered that before, but it would be logical for the women to do so. She made a note to ask Marco about it.

"So he is better, I take it?"

"Oh yes. I've heard he's already had an argument with somebody."

"With who?"

"One of us. I'm not sure what it was about, not anything important, of course. It happens. We rarely fight for very long, but sometimes things happen. I know my sultan is back when he gets cranky."

"I understand that one. I really do," Shannon replied.

"Are you wanting a tour of the honeymoon home? Marco told me that perhaps you'd like to take a walk through the gardens, and we could take the little cart over to the house or we could walk. It's about a mile and a half. I was told we'd have to take one of Marco's men, but there are a handful of us who would like to go with you if you're up to it."

"I would love to. Just as soon as I'm done here, I'm ready."

She took her mug, promising to return with the ladies.

"I'll find out who I'm supposed to take as security. I'm sure he's going to have a preference."

Marco entered the hall with four well-built younger men, and she guessed they were the Navy contingent he'd been waiting for.

"There she is, my princess," Marco said.

"I was wondering where you were. Are you going to introduce me to your friends?" Shannon asked as she stood.

One by one, they were introduced, the last one had to remove his latex gloves before he would shake hands with her.

"Sorry, we've been handling stuff I don't want to contaminate you with. But it's very nice to meet you, ma'am," the young blonde boy said.

"You guys all look so young!"

"They *are* young. They look young because I'm old. Remember, Shannon, you're marrying an old guy."

The Navy group laughed, and Shannon could tell there was quite a bit of camaraderie between all of them.

"I'm going take your suggestion, Marco, and go for a walk to find the honeymoon house. Several of the wives want to come along. I understand we're supposed to take a guard, so can you arrange that for me?"

He stepped over to her, and she could tell he wanted to grab her around the waist and press her hard against him, but wanted to show more respect in front of their new audience. He gave her a gentle peck on the cheek. "What, pray tell, are you going to do for me?"

There were whoops and hollers from the Navy men behind him. Shannon stared into Marco's eyes and whispered, "Oh, I think something involving red sashes, some wonderful creams, and maybe a bottle of whiskey this time. I sure do wish they had a hot tub here." She smiled, and his smile mirrored hers.

"As a matter of fact, they do. It's over at the Honeymoon House, but you're going to have to wait on that one."

The men continued to call out comments.

"Then I guess we'll have to do without. We'll improvise, Marco," she whispered.

"Well, you heard it yourselves, gents. My future wife is planning a party for this evening. And I'm going to be very frank, you're not invited."

SHANNON, THE WIVES, and Gary, one of Marco's security detail, walked through the jungles and garden path past fragrant flowers and vines that twisted around palm trees and other flowering trees. She could hear birds calling and remembered being told they had imported some coral-colored parrots for their event. She thought she could hear some.

"No, those are the fruit parrots. Those are green," said one of the wives.

The guard Marco had assigned had just recently detached from the military and was going to be helping run security at the Trident Towers. He stayed behind ten feet or more and checked in by a small microphone attached to his jacket every five minutes. He answered calls or questions that came over his earpiece. Shannon felt secure, although it was distracting to hear some of the squawks and the conversations said in code.

"We have a lagoon over off this way if we follow this path, and it's wonderful for swimming," one of the wives motioned.

"I want to see the house first. Can we do that?" Shannon asked.

"Of course."

About forty-five minutes later, the pathway arched to the left. Through the foliage, as they got closer and closer, a huge structure was revealed. It had a metal roof and was designed in such a way that it looked out of place on this exotic island. It contained more glass than concrete. The outside was finished in a stucco-type material that was embedded with pieces of coral and shells, giving it a pink palace look with a modern twist. The colors were stunning, and beyond the home to the side, she could see the ocean peeking through the trees.

One of the wives had a key to the front door, so she opened it and allowed Shannon to be the first one to walk in.

She felt like she was walking into a cathedral in Europe. The foyer was nearly three stories tall leading to a grand living room with windows decorated in stained glass shedding bright colors all over the marble and travertine floors. Everywhere she looked were carvings and inlay of birds, vines, flowers, and some scenes depicting the ocean surf and the pink beach beyond. There was one stunning window up high that was a sunset done in peaches and roses and reds. She was left without words.

The size of the home was enormous, yet it only had two bedrooms, one grand bedroom which was probably the master suite with a beautiful pink marble bathroom and a second on the reverse side of the house done in light gray marble, with its own electronic features such as a large screen TV and an old-fashioned music box. There were musical instruments left behind, and the bedroom also was large enough to contain a billiard table. She turned and looked back at the group from the doorway. "His and hers? A honeymoon house where he sleeps here and she sleeps there?"

The wives tittered and giggled.

One of them came up to her and said, "But isn't it nice to keep the mystery alive? Like sometimes you can be in his room, sometimes you can be in her room. The change of scenery is good for your sex life, madam."

She was very young. Shannon knew she was several years younger than her, but her bright eyes and sweet smile showed Shannon that she was indeed experienced in the art of lovemaking, as all the women in his harem were.

She winked at the young wife, adding, "You're right. I've learned something. It's variety, right?"

Several of the women giggled, pulling their saris across their mouths, and nodded their heads.

The young Navy guard frowned. "I got to see this. Do you mind?" He walked through the entrance to the gray bathroom and whistled. "The size of the closet in here is as big as my apartment back home. This is your honeymoon house? This is where you'll spend your honeymoon?" he asked.

"Indeed, it is. Pretty nice, right?"

Several of the wives had walked out to the backyard off of the lanai patio that stretched fifty feet or more before the porch covering ended. With very shallow steps, they made their way down to the sandy shore and watched the bright blue ocean undulate in the sunlight. It was one of the most beautiful views Shannon had ever seen.

There was a hammock built for two or three hanging between two palm trees to the right and a small cupola with a screened area that contained a pool, like a hot tub. "This is beautiful. I think I've died and gone to heaven," she exclaimed.

The group walked along the shoreline, noticing far out in the distance several fishing boats. One was passing by, and two were anchored. Beyond them, a large container ship slowly sailed by. Other than that, there wasn't any evidence of civilization anywhere. Several islands covered in greenery sat in a chain to the left, but no structures or power lines were seen, no boats hitched. Beneath the turquoise water, Shannon noticed a shallow area with a coral reef, which would be perfect snorkeling. She made a note to ask about getting some equipment to do that.

"So how long do people usually stay here, and who stays here?" she asked.

"It was built several years ago, about five years, I think. When he took his last wife, he had the house built so they had some privacy. Of course he's had daughters who have been married and family sometimes from the staff, depending. This is only used for people to celebrate their honeymoon. It's not a vacation home, and no children are ever allowed."

"It's just a special place just for honeymoons then?" she asked.

"Yes. Very special. Very private and very special."

They locked the house up after Shannon had a tour of the gardens. Someone had decorated the rose garden with statues of naked women, which made Shannon chuckle. The sultan's touch and choices were everywhere around them. She had not seen roses, but beneath one large water statue was a vase containing a half dozen gorgeous red, pink, and white roses, extremely fragrant and perfectly pruned. "If you wish, I have something you can clip some roses and bring back to your room. It is allowed," one of the wives said.

"Thank you. Yes, I'd like that." She asked for Shannon to point to the flowers she'd like to take, and after she was given the bouquet of half a dozen beautiful fully blooming roses and buds ready to burst, they began their trip back down the shell pathway on their way back to the palace. When the turnoff to the lagoon came up again, they decided to take that trail, and the wives showed her the beautiful swimming hole that had been created with flat soapstone slabs and rocks. They told her they often used the place for swimming and bathing.

Again, with the jungle foliage so thick around them, it was a private location. There were several paths that led into the lagoon area. "Where do these go?"

"Some of them lead back to the houses where family lives. If you go not very far in this direction, you come to the ocean again. There's a small bay there where boats that bring supplies or pleasure crafts can be docked."

"Is that where we came off the taxi?"

She shook her head no.

Shannon began walking down one particular path

until she heard the rustling sound of the surf and the waves of the ocean. Birds called, and in the jungle were sounds of scurrying small animals and birds getting out of the way as the women and their chaperone passed. Just before they came to the beach, they heard voices.

Shannon carefully hid herself behind a large palm tree and peered around to see if she could identify the people talking. She saw one of the sultan's wives speaking to a young man in rolled up dirty pants and no shirt. They appeared to be arguing, and then she burst into tears, hiding her face. "Oh dear. That is not allowed," said one of the older wives.

"Who is she?" asked Shannon. She didn't recognize her.

"That's Sarika. She is one of his newer wives. She comes from another island, formerly an island kingdom that was dissolved, absorbed by India some years ago. Her family came into disfavor with the Indian government, and she was orphaned when she lost her parents when she was small. The sultan took her in. Because, well—"

Shannon could see there was something delicate the wife didn't want to say.

One of the other wives spoke up. "She was defiled. Victim of rape. It is difficult to be married into a good home, a good house if this has happened. The sultan took her as one of his wives."

"That must be a brother or something. Maybe she does have family left," said Shannon.

One of the older wives motioned for them to leave, and as Shannon was the last, she turned around and saw the young couple embrace in an erotic kiss that was not remotely familial.

She knew she was going to have to let Marco know about this right away.

CHAPTER 9

I WAS IN the middle of discussing several items with the sweep team from the Navy when Shannon and several of the wives bolted in and came running straight for me.

"Marco! You have to hear about this!"

The women behind Shannon were whispering amongst themselves and discussing with other members of the staff. I immediately put my hands up and stopped all the conversation.

"Whoa, whoa, whoa! Let's hold it right there. If we have some information about what's going on, I want it said in private. I do not want gossip to be spread throughout this kingdom. It's important that we do this the right way. Nobody leaves this room until Shannon tells her story. Do you understand?"

My security detail had stood as soon as the ladies entered, ready for whatever was to come next. The wives immediately nodded their heads, as well as three of the housekeeping staff who had been waiting on us during our meeting. I took Shannon's hand and sat her next to me on the big red leather couch.

"Okay, Shannon, tell me what's going on."

She caught her breath, her face pale white with what I took to be fear.

"Well, we went over to the honeymoon house, and oh, Marco, it's lovely."

"I'm sure it is. But let's get to the story, okay?"

"Yes, yes, of course. We walked over to the bathing pool, I think they call it the lagoon, and it had several trails that went off in different directions, and I was just exploring one of the trails. They told me it led to the beach. We walked through the jungle forest, and gradually, I could hear the water and sounds of the surf, and then we heard voices. So very carefully, we listened and crept through the foliage until we saw two people on the beach talking, a man and a woman. It appeared the man had arrived by boat, a small boat. Their conversation was very heated—looked like arguing."

"Who? Are these people from this household?" I demanded, needing to get to the point.

Shannon looked to the group of wives.

"Yes. One of the sultan's wives and another gentleman—they were both young." Again, she looked to the women. "I believe she is one of his newer wives."

"How do you know this? Did you recognize her?"

"No, I was told. But we assumed she was speaking to her brother."

I stood up and put my hands on my hips and turned. "So? That's not unusual. What made you think it was suspicious activity?" I studied the women, cowering in the corner.

"Because—"

"Sir," one of the younger wives spoke up boldly. "Whether or not she was with her brother, it makes no difference. It is forbidden for her to speak to a man unaccompanied. This is not allowed."

"Who is this woman? Is she one of his wives? Are you sure?" I asked her.

"Her name is Meera, and she has been married to the sultan about five years, came to live with us then," she told me.

I was furious that a member of his party walked without an accompaniment to the other side of the island. And since I knew that area to be a major pickup and drop off area, it was also unsafe. I wondered if he was there to assist her in an escape.

Shannon spoke up again.

"They were arguing, Marco. We started to move away, and when I turned around to look at them, they had embraced and they kissed. And it wasn't like they were brother and sister. It was an intimate kiss. Swear to God, Marco, it's not my imagination."

Although I was glad that we were getting closer to perhaps the bottom of the plot, I was still struggling with a reason or motivation for the sultan's poisoning. But Shannon apparently thought they were connected. I knew I had to do some checking with the sultan and his number one wife. But I threw down some ultimatums to the room first.

"Who knows her well?"

The wife who spoke to me earlier stepped forward. "She sometimes confides in me."

"Is her reputation solid in this household? Have you had any problems with her in the past?"

All three of the women again answered without speaking, by shaking their heads no.

"Do you know who she was talking to? Does he work here in the kingdom?"

"No. But I do believe he could have been her former betrothed. They were promised to each other as children through their families. I don't know all of the story."

"I need to talk to her right away. I would like one of you to go to the harem quarters and see if you can find her. Bring her to me. Do not tell anybody. Just tell her that the sultan would like to see her, but bring her here to me."

As perhaps the youngest of the three scampered off

down the hallway toward their quarters, I addressed the other two.

"Not a word of this to anyone. I'm sure the sultan and his number one will ask you questions, and that's okay. But there is to be no gossip, and until she's thoroughly vetted, she may not be the suspect, but neither is she innocent. Do you understand?"

Again, they agreed.

"Everyone stays right here until we find her. No one leaves this room." I addressed the wait staff as well. "Unfortunately, I can't let you go, either. You've seen more than I wanted you to see here, and you're going to have to stay until we get this resolved. And no one is to leave the island, is that clear?"

I turned to my Navy boys, who agreed.

"We'll get the word out, Marco," said Darius, who I permitted to leave.

"Does anyone know anything else about this wife and the man she may be speaking to today?"

One of the waitstaff stepped forward. "The man she was with was likely her betrothed, many years ago. As children, they were committed to each other, as has been said. I believe he has been recently returned, having been sent to the military. I believe I overheard this when we were unloading supplies. Perhaps he feels he has a right to claim her."

"But she's married to the sultan. That's a contract."

I was worried that breaking the marriage contract was grounds for imprisonment or worse in this society. The sultan didn't have a prison on his island, but the Indian authorities would certainly intervene, and her life would be made quite difficult.

We didn't have to wait long. The wife I sent to retrieve Meera came back, holding her hand, bringing her in tow. They stopped just in front of me.

Meera was glancing around her, at the congregation of the American men seated at the table with Shannon, her sister-wives, and me. She looked genuinely confused. Speaking to her sister-wife, it was translated for us.

"She says she was summoned to meet with the sultan. She came specifically to meet him here. Is this the meeting place or—?"

"Have a seat please," I interrupted, motioning to the chair.

She delicately set her frame down, her back ramrod stiff and her eyes frightened and unable to contact mine or any of the other sister-wives. At last, she placed her hands in her lap and looked down, waiting for instructions.

I motioned to the other wife to translate for us, and she quickly rose, standing beside Meera.

"You were seen with a young man at the beach today. Who is this person, and why did you disobey the sultan's rules about wandering the island without protection?"

She waited for the translation and then began. "He is a friend from many years ago, before I was married. He has been insisting that I meet with him. I did not invite him. I requested that he leave."

"But you met with him anyway," I insisted.

"He found me, threatened to make a scene if I wouldn't meet with him in private. I had to take that risk for his own safety, as well as mine. I knew if he were caught he would get in trouble. So I agreed to meet him at the dock."

I knew it was possible, of course, but I needed to find out if she was involved in the poisoning.

"Is he responsible for poisoning the sultan?"

I noted that the idea was foreign to her, but as she considered it, I could see some clarity come to her face. Then she put her hand to her mouth, bent over, and began to cry.

"Where is he now?"

The sister-wife asked her three or four times the same question, and Meera refused to answer. Behind me, I heard rustling and noted that Number One had entered. I turned, backing away so she could address the woman herself. She stepped within two feet of the young wife, waited until the girl looked up to her, and then slapped her across the face. I didn't want to physically restrain his number one wife, but a fight would risk everyone else's existence if they got involved in it. I moved to block his number one and asked the young wife where her friend was.

Number One blurted out. "He lives in the camp down by the docks, isn't that right, Meera?"

The translator spoke to her and then, in perfect English, gave the bride's answer.

"I am so sorry, sir. I have broken the rules, and I am not worthy of all that has been given me. He is not well, and I only thought if I met with him, perhaps I could stop him from doing something I was afraid of, or perhaps hurting me or one of the other wives. It didn't occur to me that he would be the person to try to take the sultan's life. I really didn't think he would do that."

Number One spoke up, spitting as she did so, showing her disgust. "So you sit here and tell us that even when the sultan was poisoned, you didn't think to tell us about this person? The person you thought could create harm? His life was in grave danger, but you never thought to try to protect him with this information? Meera, where are your loyalties? Where is your moral compass?"

"I am so sorry. What is he going to do to me?" Meera asked, her eyes wide and filling with tears.

"There will be no mercy shown you here," said

Number One. "This will be taken up with the Indian authorities, if you are involved."

"But I didn't know he would—"

"You failed to report it," I added. "You are not to be trusted, Meera."

"It will go better for you if you help Marco find him. After that, it's up to the Indian authorities. I am not sure what this will entail or what they will do. But we need to find him. It'll be way more dangerous for you if we do not, and it's very dangerous for him, either way."

"I will. I promise to help you find him. I owe that to the sultan," she said through her tears.

The rest of the afternoon was spent organizing a team to scour the sea village across the channel, looking for Meera's former boyfriend. I sent one from the Naval research team to verify the presence of any strychnine at his home, if we found it, and I had several others accompany them in addition to one of the other wives. My men were instructed to get in, find him, and get him out before they were noticed.

Again I admonished them to not discuss the situation with anyone and then dismissed them.

Shannon was beside herself.

"How did he even get in touch with her? You know, Marco, she must have had help from somebody on the outside?"

Number One stepped into our conversation.

"We do occasionally receive deliveries and visitors, and he could have posed as one of those. We have been bringing in lots of fresh food, now that the kitchen is safe. The sooner we locate him, the better we can find out how he did it."

I now had a whole team of other people to interview, families of the staff who worked there, some of the delivery people. We had easily a hundred people left to interview. Time was not our friend, and until then, the sultan was being guarded round the clock. I had been told he was beginning to object to all the scrutiny and his lack of privacy.

That was a good sign.

The sultan was up and about, speaking with several of his wives and the staff, and looked to be much better. His skin coloring was nearly back to normal. He said his bones ached, but he told me that was his condition before he got sick.

At dusk, the team brought the unfortunate young man to us, with the report that he'd confessed to the poisoning out of jealousy and revenge. The young man was pushed down onto the marble floor and thrown at the sultan's feet.

The sultan yelled at him with a voice that rattled windows in the great hall. "You come into my household and threaten these women, these people, their livelihoods. You threaten me? All I have done is help Meera. I was there for her when you were gone. You abandoned her after you defiled her. What would have happened if you'd left her with child?"

The boy mumbled to the floor. "But she was to be my wife. She was promised—"

"You took permission where you were given none. You took what was not yours. I could have you rot in prison for the rest of your life if I decided to. What kind of a life for her is that? Bringing you water and fruits and candies and screwing all the guards at the prison for the chance to see you? Just so she could have a few minutes alone with you? How dare you place her in such danger. I saved her from an outcast life of poverty, and this is how you show your respect for what I have done?"

He didn't look up but kept his body touching the floor, his forehead kissing the marble, his hands at the sides of his head, knees tucked, his butt in the air.

"I am sorry, my sultan. I am so sorry."

"I am not your sultan. I am merely the person who showed compassion for someone who had been harmed by your actions. She doesn't belong with you, but thanks to you, she will no longer have a home here, food to eat, or the sisterhood around her. She will be cast out again. You have done this."

The man on the floor began to wail. The sultan got

up and was going to kick him in the gut but looked at me as he tried to get his balance to make the kick. I was not encouraging. In fact, I really didn't want him to do any physical damage to the man or it would lighten our case.

"What can I do? Please, what can I do to save Meera from that fate?" the man mumbled.

I stepped in, hoping to calm the waters.

"You can help her situation if you cooperate and tell us how you managed the poisoning? Tell me the truth, and you have a chance to save some of your dignity."

The sultan flopped down on the leather couch with a growl. He acted like a wounded bear.

"I came on the island and lived by the lagoon for two days before I saw Meera. I planned to take her back to my village, but she rejected me, told me to leave. I stole from the garbage, foraged for food for myself. I believed I could convince her to leave with me, but she refused, over and over again. Then I watched as your helper baited the box for the rats by the scrapyard, and I realized that if I took that poison I could use it to make you sick. I stole the box and pried open. I waited for the right opportunity and mixed it in with some cooked peppers and curry that were cooling in the outside kitchen area. I had been told it was your favorite dish. I only wanted to make you sick, I didn't intend to take your life."

The whole room drew their attention to the sultan.

He surveyed the faces of his family and staff, his eyes finally resting on Meera. "What would you have me do, Meera?"

"You will never trust me again. I have broken my promise, and I don't think you should ever trust me to be in your house. I have greatly enjoyed it here. I wish I had not acted behind your back to meet him, but I promise I never meant to cause you harm. You have been good to me."

"Do you love him?"

"My sultan, sadly, no. It is delusional on his part to think that I would spend a life with him. But my mistake was not informing you or your Number One. And for that, I should pay."

"I regret that you will have to leave my household, Meera. I only hope that you will at some future date learn how to live on the right path. But I cannot take the chance you would harm me or anyone else in this household. You have lost your opportunity and your position."

The sultan looked over at the young man. "You will be taken to the police in Cochin, and you will be turned over to them for a trial and sentencing. If Meera testifies on your behalf, perhaps that can help your situation. But I wash my hands of you, and if you ever were to return to this kingdom again, we will not be so lenient. But I will not push for a harsh sentence."

The young man's jaw was rigid, anger and resentment seething from his eyes. "You are a snake," he said to the sultan. The crowd was aghast.

"You reject the gift of compassion? You truly are a troubled young man and not worthy to take a bride from anywhere. Perhaps you shall die like one, my son. And you shall never have the love of your dreams, but you will die knowing that you ruined someone else's life as well. For Meera no longer will have a life coveted by so many. You've destroyed her chance at happiness. You can die knowing that you gave me the poison, but you poisoned Meera's life too."

CHAPTER 10

S HANNON SPENT THE following day attending to last-minute preparations for the wedding. As the Navy team continued sweeping through the island properties, they set up monitoring devices and camera surveillance that could be maintained and operated off the island, a highly sophisticated system that Marco had found for him and agreed to update and monitor for as long as the sultan desired.

The sultan had recovered remarkably well. Most of the laughter and happiness of the household was gone, however. Everyone was keenly aware of the impact the sultan's health had on the family. And Shannon realized for the first time that he really was the hub where all the spokes of the wheel joined. And he was not going to be able to quickly transfer that to anyone else. Even his sons were not trained to take over running a kingdom.

It was the one thing Shannon felt the sultan had

ignored, and now that he was faced with an impending end, there wasn't the time to really fix it. So the household was filled with sadness and thoughts of the inevitable demise of the great man. She knew her future husband, even though he would do anything for the sultan, also was incapable of truly fixing this. There was nothing to be done now.

She spoke to Marco privately when they were alone. They were planning to leave the following day.

"Has he given any thought to what will happen once he goes? I mean, who will keep this household, who will run it?" she asked.

"I've tried to talk to him about it, Shannon. He refuses to discuss it. I know he doesn't want to send everybody into chaos, but I'm afraid he's resigned himself to someone else solving it for him. And as close as I am to him, even I can't do it. He's not going to give the power to either one of his sons or his wives, especially now."

"So what'll happen with Meera and her wanna-be lover?" Shannon asked.

"He's facing many, many years in prison. Perhaps some kind of clemency would be granted after the sultan's death, but there's no guarantee on that. The government of India, who is responsible for certain security matters of the kingdom, since it's within its sphere, really doesn't have the capacity to handle it. I'm guessing there are politicians in India who have their sights on the island someday. This whole way of life that we're witnessing is probably also going to fade, just like he will."

"Then I'm glad he will die before he has to see all that happen," she said.

"These are the stories of all the great maharajas and islands that are in the Indian Ocean as, one by one, they became hotels or luxury resorts, places where the rich and famous could rent a castle, a villa, or a palace for themselves and their entourage. There will always be people who want that. But the number of people who are in this world able to afford maintaining it and keeping it, that number's dwindling. There used to be a thousand islands with kingdoms on them. And they used to pitch wars against each other hundreds of years ago. Now, they're just paper tigers."

Shannon felt her eyes moisten as she mourned, in advance, the death of a lifestyle.

"We have to learn to adapt, sweetheart. We have to learn to take what the world gives us and, if anything, learn from this. We can't be stuck in one place, treasuring a lifestyle or trying to hang on to something that is not going to last. We have to be adaptable. We have to notice the trends and the people out there, and at some point, we have to know, just like the song says, when to hold them and when to fold them. I don't think it's possible for the sultan to ever be able to make that decision. And some people are just like that."

He gently pressed his palm against her cheek.

"But don't grieve, Shannon. Enjoy what's here. Enjoy the fantasy, the life of a small little clutch of family members, a dying kingdom. Enjoy it, and then like a butterfly, let it go. Let it fly off."

Shannon was reminded of what she had to do with one of her friends who was cleaning out her mother's closets and things after she passed away.

"I'm thinking about my friend Judy and what we had to do after her mother died. She kept saying over and over again, why did mom not get rid of all this stuff? Her mother just didn't want to come to the point where she had to let go of this stuff, she just couldn't do it, and so she passed away leaving that to somebody else. I don't want to do that to our kids. I don't want to make them have to go through that."

"I've experienced that going through things I had to ship home when I had someone on the teams who passed. It was left up to me to decide what to keep and what not to. Most of it, I kept because it wasn't my decision, and I figured if my SEAL buddy kept it, there was a reason in there somewhere, although most of the time it wasn't clear. I remember talking to a widow when it had been several weeks since her husband passed away. I called on her. I was asked to by the Navy to see if I could help, and she took me outside to her backyard, which was filled with sand, piles of wood here and there, plants in pots, and some that were needing to be planted. A huge concrete mixer and bags of concrete covered in plastic was the focal point of the backyard. So much stuff the kids couldn't even play out there."

"Did you help?"

"Yup. When he went off with SEAL Team 3, that fateful day six months before, it was supposed to be a temporary TDI, and he'd be back in a week or two. Except he never came back. And he left this big yard filled with a mess. His unfinished project."

"So what did you do?"

"I promised her we'd take care of it. I asked her if she would allow me to complete it for him. And so we got together a regular party, you know, one of my SEAL team parties. We got about twenty guys, their wives, their friends, the kids, everybody got into it. We had kids bringing in pallets of lawn and laying them out and stamping on them, watering plants. We had wives hauling wheelbarrows, digging holes, and trimming trees. We had some of the youngsters hauling big black bags of cuttings and trash out to the curb to be picked up. It took us all weekend, but in the end, on Sunday night, we all stood there in the middle of his garden, and we knew that we had finished his vision."

Shannon had a hard time stifling back tears. "That's one of the most amazing stories I think I've ever heard you tell, Marco. I can't imagine how grateful she must have been."

"She was. And a few weeks later, in the team building, there was a big fight."

"What over?"

"Well, you know how it is, when one warrior passes away, the rest of us take it upon ourselves to take care of the wife and kids. We knew he'd want someone else to raise his children who had the same ethos and honor he did. And so within the next few weeks, it was decided what the pecking order would be. We gave the chosen man our best, and he spent the summer wooing the widow, asked her to marry him, and then did."

"That's the way it is with police and fire, too, sometimes; I've talked to widows who almost have to refuse men from their husband's force stopping by bringing flowers and casseroles and little gifts for the kids. I had one woman I interviewed who was angry about it."

"Well, that's because she probably hadn't finished grieving. It's hard to let go and to think about a future. Especially since the whole center of your life is gone. I had to do that on a limited basis with Emily. I didn't have time to grieve. I was still running missions at that time, and then I decided to do something else with my life. I jumped into my relationship with Rebecca, and I was off to the races again. This time, Shannon, you came to me. And that's probably the only way it would've happened. You healed me."

"I think what you're saying is we all have to find our futures, and that means everybody here at the palace, they'll have stories to tell. The kids will talk about it, won't they?" she asked him.

"Yep, there'll be lots of stories told, and some of them will even be true."

He put his arm around her. "I think getting married here is the greatest gift we could give the sultan. I was so worried he wasn't going to make it, but now that he is, we're putting double and triple into his safety here so that we can have our day and the sultan can have his one last party. He doesn't want to say it's a goodbye party. He wants to say that it's our wedding celebration, but it really is a goodbye party, Shannon. And I can't think of anybody else I'd rather walk through that doorway to the future with than you. Lots of stories to tell our children, right?"

"Absolutely. Thank you, Marco. That puts it all in perspective."

Saying goodbye that next day was difficult for Shannon. There were many tears shed and still some uneasy nerves. The sultan himself appeared to be in a great mood, starting to get back his usual laughing self, but nobody else was really feeling a tremendous amount of joy, especially since Marco and Shannon were leaving. But Marco had assured everybody that the detail he was leaving behind would lay down their lives for any one of them. The kingdom had been way more vulnerable than he thought, and they were going to do everything in their power to make sure they were protected, but not feeling like they were cooped up in a military prison somewhere. Shannon knew that security was an issue for the women.

Sultan's wife number one confided in Shannon the day they left that he promised her he was not going to marry again. Of course, the two women knew that he didn't have much chance of living very long past the wedding, but it was important for him to tell her that she was his most important wife, his number one wife, and that he was done marrying.

Shannon realized it was way more important to wife number one than it was to anybody else. Maybe it was his way of telling her he had always loved her and perhaps loved her most. The household had been turned into a hospital of sorts with the sultan's treatments, and they knew he was going to be sick while receiving some of these treatments, so rather than spending time worrying about sexual favors, she knew the women were going to be more like nursemaids for him. Which was what his needs were.

They took the helicopter up and away after Marco gave his last-minute instructions to his team leader, and everyone waved as the two of them ascended into the sky. They took a limo shuttle to Mumbai where they caught a commercial liner back to New York and then took the flight down to Tampa. It was a long day when they arrived back at Indian Rocks Beach, but as soon as they got off the plane, she felt she was truly home. It was an adventure she would never forget. It would heighten the tension but also the enjoyment of the wedding. It was the acknowledgment of a life well lived for a man worthy of praise. And it was something Marco wanted to do with her by his side. That was the most important thing of all.

On the second day they were home, they drove out at sunset to watch the beautiful orange and yellow and rose-colored clouds, sitting in the shell of their home which had been closed in but wasn't complete. The balcony had yet to be built but the platform was there. And that's where they sat and ate some Indian takeout they'd picked up along the way, watching the sunset and the waves and the beach.

She angled her head a little bit and was considering something when Marco asked her what she was thinking about.

"I don't know whether I like pink sand or white sand. I think I like the white sand better."

"My dear, if that is your opinion, you are commanded to keep it to yourself."

"Yes, sir. Anything you want."

"Anything?" he asked.

She held his face between her hands, kissed him, and said, "Anything."

CHAPTER 11

ABOUT SEVEN DAYS after we returned back into Florida, we were finally able to have the groundbreaking ceremony I'd wanted to have for nearly six months. There had been so much going on, especially with the trip to the kingdom. Everything had gotten delayed, and it was looking like we might have to postpone the whole thing until after the wedding sometime in January or February.

What I wasn't prepared for was the fact that everyone came together on this thing, the contractors really pushed themselves to try to do things ahead of time. It was the most cooperative and successful planning and start to a project I'd ever experienced. And I'd done plenty of complexes.

Sam's input was invaluable. Whenever we ran into some kind of an issue we had to solve, he was the first person we called. We asked him how it would impact a disabled person, how would someone who needed to cook and clean and rest and use the bathroom be able to use a space or a stairway or a ramp, and I think because it was centered on the disabled the project almost became a living, breathing thing. We were honoring something that was bigger and way beyond ourselves. It was a wonderful lesson in how well people could work together.

We did have our detractors. We occasionally got hit pieces written in magazines and newspapers, but whenever they went digging, they couldn't find any dirt, because everything was not being done for profit. And we could prove it too. Today, as I stood next to Shannon, we had the governor, the mayors of several little beach towns, the mayor of Tampa, the heads of our local police and first responders, the fire department, and presidents of three local hospitals all working in sync, where they were normally competitors to each other.

I wanted the picture of all of us standing together with the shovel in my hand so that I could remember there was a day in December before Christmas when the whole community came together. Each of us took a shovel full of dirt and tossed it into the center, the crowd clapping and the photographs clicking. We all went to dinner at a catered Oddfellows Hall, overlooking the ocean in St. Petersburg.

The place had been an old fisherman hall, back in

the days when early settlers built the coastal towns, set up their big houses, and conducted their fishing operations on individual piers, depending on what they could afford at the time. Most of the buildings that were used in those days were gone, but this one, built in the 1840s, remained. I was told it was the only one that did. Hurricanes had a way of leveling the playing field and just like roofs for houses weren't expected to last more than ten or twelve years, no matter what the material, piers and big wooden halls would always fall victim to angry wind and rain.

We were exhausted from all the preparations, and even though some of our civic leaders wanted to continue to party into the night, Shannon and I said our goodbyes and left.

I was looking forward to my first day back at the office.

"Boss!" said Dax. "I tried to straighten things up as best I could, but I'm just not talented like you are. I'm afraid you're going to find things a mess. I wasn't quite sure what day you'd be in. I mean, everything's in good shape. It's just not clean."

"I'm okay with that, Dax. I know you guys are working hard. Let's just see what you got. And judging from the pile of papers on my desk, looks like I better start at the top and go down."

"Well, we tried to send you messages on everything, and we've made a booklet of the change orders and the contracts. I really think you ought to review all those first. Your CFO signed and arranged for certain advanced payments that you agreed to, but I really want you to look at all the contracts. And maybe you'll see something we all missed."

"Sounds good to me."

She motioned for me to go into the conference room since my desk didn't have very much room for stacking files and going through paperwork. I had forgotten how beautiful the room was, looking out into the blue ocean, with the big billowy white and gray clouds out in the distance. I could see we were going to have rain soon, and I had noted a large population of dragonflies around Shannon's house and around our new home site, which always indicated there was going to be a change in weather soon. We even had butter-flies this time of year, but I knew they would be done very soon.

She plopped several folders that were tabbed and held together with brads right in the center of the table in front of me.

"There you go. I've got all the underground orders, all the subcontractors and the general engineering contracts for the project. On a separate file over here, I've got all their employment requirements that the county has asked us to make sure they adhere to. We want to hire veterans as much as possible, and we are to hire long-term unemployed for spaces we can."

"I understand. I knew that was going to be the case, and I totally approve."

"And then this book over here, the brown one, has a copy of all the building permits we've pulled, and I have tabs for each of the phases. You heard about the electrical contractor, right?"

"Yes, I think you told me."

"These guys are amazing. I mean they're like 'can we come over and just do this and can we get compensation to make an order.' I think they have pretty much all the materials they're going to need for the whole project. They've rented a storage facility in Tampa so they could store everything, and it's guarded twenty-four seven. I didn't realize this, but there have been a recent spate of break-ins at warehouses for construction yards, with supplies being limited. There's a pretty healthy trade in stealing other people's stuff."

I laughed at her commentary. "Other people's stuff, huh?"

"You know what I mean."

"I'll look these over. Are you going to be around in case I have questions?"

"I am, and if I'm not," she pulled out her cell phone, "just give me a ring."

"How are the wedding plans coming?"

Dax blushed before she added, "Well, we kind of were waiting for yours to be over first, because everything had to be working around this project and that trip. We've kind of put it on hold, just doing minimal amounts of things."

"You have a date?"

"Not yet, Boss. We're going to do that soon. I think we want to look and see what you guys do, and maybe we'll get some ideas."

I threw my head back and laughed at that suggestion. I didn't want to make fun of her, but I knew there wasn't going to be any possibility her wedding was going to look anything like ours. But I knew she liked to dream, and I considered it a good thing.

I went through over half of the early project permits, and I read all the proposals for contracts that weren't signed yet. We tried to do a competitive bidding process, but there were certain cases where it was going to be particularly good to choose one contractor over another. The biggest determination would be whether or not they had disabled employees. We had a steel fabricator who climbed all over tall office buildings in downtown Tampa as they were being built, ten- and twelve-story skyscrapers, and was disabled. He had no legs and used a rigging system to get up and down off of the buildings. I had read an article about that guy, and even though his price was a little higher than the two other bids we got, I put a note to make sure he was the one who got the job. And I didn't want anyone pressuring him to lower his price.

I received a call from Senator Campbell in Washington, DC.

"Senator, what can I do you for?"

"I understand you had quite a party yesterday. Everything going well?"

"Yes, I've got enough paperwork to choke a horse, but nothing like what you guys have, of course."

"Oh, tell me about it. Our rules for the budget committee this year are nearly eight inches thick. Those are just the rules. The regulations are, I think, about as thick as well. Honest to God, I think we'd be a greater country if we didn't put so much in writing."

"Damn, Senator, don't let anybody hear you say that."

"Oh, I'm well aware. You know, I learned a lot about butterflies after you took those pictures of some of the butterflies you have there in Florida. I was reading that the monarch has to eat milkweed. If the monarch lays her eggs on anything but a milkweed plant, the little baby caterpillar will die because that's the only plant it can eat. I got to thinking about that when I was looking at the piles of paper I had to send off to the shredder. After we review it and mark things up, then we have to get rid of it in a secure manner. But as I saw that huge cart, taking two big, strong guys to push, I thought to myself, we're just like monarch butterflies. We live on paperwork, right?"

"That's funny. Well, as long as you don't eat it, that is."

"It's the stuff we do. We live on it. I don't have to eat it to live on it."

"So how's your family? And you run into any more hotspots?"

"Well, I have to say I was a little disappointed that you weren't going to Nigeria. It's not gotten any better, but we could have used your intel, and it was good cover for some of our guys, but I don't blame you, and it's not exactly something that's going to work itself out right away. So yeah, it's still there, new ones coming all along. We've got some issues with drugs and human trafficking, just like before, but now we've run across several celebrity-type militia men in several of those countries who are targeting wealthy Saudis and European businessmen. Even a Russian oligarch. Did you read about that?"

"I did. And their Wagner group wasn't even able to help."

"Damn right. So there's big money in going after people like that. I think the trade is changing a bit. And high-value targets... I mean, let's face it, Marco. If somebody could kidnap the president of the United

States, don't you think somebody might pay some money instead of telling everybody we don't negotiate with terrorists?"

I thought about that for a second. It was a horrible idea, but desperate times were creating desperate people.

"Well, until 9/11, nobody thought they would've flown planes into buildings and have them coordinated so well. At each level, they seem to up the game a bit, don't they, Senator?"

"It's hard to combat that, which means you're probably in a pretty good field. I mean, we're going to need guys like you forever. The world isn't going to go back to some utopian little small-town farm corncob pipe dream with everybody eating apple pie and vegetables out of their garden, right? We live in dangerous times. And the best we can do for our wives and daughters and families, the innocents, is to keep them prepared. Keep talking about it. We aren't going to be able to get them all."

"But they aren't going to be able to get all of us, either. And there are enough people like you and me, Senator. We're never going to quit."

"Okay, well, I'm going to try to get down and see you before you go overseas again, and you did get our RSVP for the wedding?"

"Yes, I saw it there. Is there anybody I forgot to invite that you think I should?"

"Well, knowing how you plan a party and knowing how the sultan is, I don't suppose you would mind one more couple. Would you mind inviting my son-in-law?"

"Your son-in-law? I don't think I've met him."

"Oh, he's on our committee. He graduated from law school but had a specialty in business, sharp kid. Now don't steal him, Marco, because we need him on the committee. But his jaw still drops when he breezes past the president or the vice president, and I think he would be tickled pink if he could come to that wedding. Of course, I'm paying for everything. I'm not allowing the sultan to bankroll that."

"I didn't know he was offering that. Really?"

"Yes, he did. Now don't tell anybody, because I don't know if he's offered it to others. But Lillian and I, we're really looking forward to your wedding, and I really think I want this show of respect for the sultan, in light of his health. And you do know that I know he's on his last legs?"

"I figured. Not much gets by you, Senator."

"So his name is Dan Shay, and you can send him the invitation in care of the committee. Don't put any stupid notes on it like you forgot or anything like that. I'll just handle that myself and claim I have no idea why it came late. Maybe I'll tell him that it was there all along and I forgot to give it to him or something. But anyway, my daughter and my son-in-law would be forever grateful if they could come."

"You got it. So tell me about Africa. Who are the players then, anybody we've known from before?"

"Well, you did a pretty good job on the last bunch there, and we've had fairly good cooperation with a few of the militia leaders, bringing them some business. They're all anxious to get off the watch list and be able to do business in the United States. But the crazies are coming in. I think they get hopped up on something, and I'm not into that, so I have no idea what it is. The CIA tells us that it's a good thing and a bad thing. We have some of the bad guys dying from Fentanyl as well. But these people are ruthless. They are not necessarily... they're just plain, ordinary garden variety criminals, but they get worse and worse. They're not doing it to protest or demand something. They're just doing it because they can, because they love to cheat and steal and ruin people's lives. If they could bring down a government or two, it's like a notch in their belt. Crazy people, really crazy people."

"So it sounds like maybe next year I might have another mission or two."

"You could be right. Don't hold your breath, though, but in my book, Marco, you're the best. I know there's competition, but there's no substitute for the best."

I returned a call from Dr. Tramel, who had left a message while I was on the phone with the senator.

"Marco, I'm just calling to give you an update. It appears that all his blood work is normal. And I've been in close contact with your Navy team over there, and they haven't seen a trace of strychnine pop into the palace for about ten days. So they were asking me if they should maybe come home. They're not my team, but because I think this particular scare is over, it might be a good idea. But it's up to you."

"Yeah, I think they can come home. What does the sultan want?"

"Oh my gosh, I'm trying to get him to go on a diet. He's feeling pretty good about himself, and he eats too much fat and too much Western food for his Indian insides. That little problem with them with the yellow curry kind of took his appetite away from curry for a while, but it'll probably come back. But he's eating steak and mashed potatoes and all kinds of things I guess you introduced him to here in Florida. He doesn't much like fish, but he loves crab. I understand they've been flying over blue crabs and grouper and all kinds of things so he could keep his Florida vacation going a little bit longer. It's kind of funny when you think about it, though."

"I get you. Well, I think he should enjoy himself.

His ETA still about a month, two months?"

"I think he might have a little longer than that, but it all depends on what happens. He might get a cold, flu, or COVID. I'm most worried about the wedding and the crowd there. I'm not worried about the crowd turning on him and trying to kill him or anything, but I'm worried about what he could pick up. You're going to have people from all over the world there, Marco. You know that, right?"

"I do. And I noticed you're not on the reservation list, so are you coming or not?"

"I've got a conflict, but I think I'm going to try to make it. I don't think my wife will, but I'll come. I feel like I should. I want to give him a checkup, and I also want to double-check the lab in Mumbai."

"The lab? Why?"

"Well, I've understood there is a Chinese concern that has been purchasing laboratories, and we had a group here in Tampa try to purchase a string of labs. They do a lot of DNA testing. We're kind of concerned about the medical database that's being created by some of these organizations. I just want to walk through the lab and actually look at them, because since this transfer happened about two weeks ago, the communication's been totally different. They're not as quick to get back to me, and I'm not getting my questions answered. So I'm going to stop by for a day and just do a tour, just have them show me what they do. They send out these medical devices and kits, and I recommended them to someone who was doing some work in South America, and the kits were a mess. They came partially broken, incomplete. It was bad. And I think the guy spent over ten thousand dollars ordering this stuff. So something's happened over there, and I'm going to check it out."

"Well, I don't like the sound of that, Doc. You better go with somebody."

"A couple of your guys there said they'd be happy to do it. And I think that's what I'll do. Thanks, if you can allow that to happen."

"No problem. I'm all for it. So will I see you before the wedding or are you just going to show up?"

"No, I think I'll see you there. You take care. If you hear anything concerning the sultan, because I'm not sure he tells me everything… If you get any information from any of those wives that love you so much—"

"Watch it, Doc. You know I'm not that way."

"Yes, I know, but they might tell you something they may not tell me. So if you get an inkling about anything, you let me know, okay?"

"Absolutely. It's a deal. I'm going to sit down with you. We'll put our feet in the water and have a nice longneck beer when I see you next. How about that?"

"You got it, Marco. Take care."

CHAPTER 12

AFTER THE GROUNDBREAKING ceremony, Shannon noticed a big uptick in "drop by" appearances, unannounced by media and their staff. Videos and photographs were taken at the site as they began their first pours. There were offers of TV interviews, and even Shannon's former Tampa television station begged her to come back and do some exclusive interviews. She was going to ask Rebecca if perhaps she'd like to do that, figuring it might be good for her to get out of the office.

She'd noticed Marco's ex had been not her usual self and appeared to be mildly depressed. At best, quiet. But she wasn't sure and certainly didn't want to ask.

With all the increased scrutiny, Marco wisely put extra details on all of them. Shannon was getting used to the idea of waking up and going for a run on the beach with two former Navy SEALs at her side. In her old days, she would have relished the opportunity to get to know some handsome, young fit men. But now it made her feel embarrassed. They were extremely well-behaved, and she suspected that they knew exactly how she felt.

Marco must be having a field day watching me.

There were new faces around the office, as several additional staffers were added, especially to deal with the public scrutiny. They hired a media copy editor to handle press releases. Various officials from all the little towns up and down the Gulf Coast made an appearance, had to be seen shaking Marco's hand with the cranes and cement trucks in the background.

While she was pleased that support for the Trident Towers had skyrocketed, she wasn't so sure she was ready for all the notoriety.

When she came into the office in the morning, Rebecca was waiting for her.

"Can I have a little bit of your attention please? Alone?" Rebecca said, eyeing the handsome fellow to Shannon's right.

He was quick to understand without making them feel awkward.

"Listen, let me go get you guys some waters or do you want coffee or tea?" he asked.

"Coffee, and I think, Rebecca, you want coffee, as well?"

"Absolutely. Overdo it with the cream."

After her security detail left, Rebecca leaned into Shannon, whispering, "How do you get them to do that? Nice as all get out, handsome, built, and just decent. You know, in my younger days, I wouldn't have been interested in that type. Now that I'm older? I could do without the drama."

"I've heard stories, Rebecca."

"I'll bet you have. But, boy, I enjoyed myself way back then."

Shannon smiled. "Come on in. We'll leave the door open so he can bring our coffee."

They situated themselves on either side of Shannon's messy desk. Their coffee was served, the door closed, and they were finally alone.

"What's on your mind, Rebecca?"

Shannon was wondering if she was going to make a request about the wedding and the fact that she did not get an invitation. She was not looking forward to having to explain it to her but promised herself she would own up and be straightforward. Rebecca was not welcome at the sultan's palace, and Marco didn't want to have anything to do with her, either.

"I'm sure you've noticed things here have changed quite a bit. And I'm happy with that. I'm happy for all of you." Rebecca hesitated.

"But you are not happy here?" Shannon asked her.

"Well, I do have a history quite different than

yours, Shannon. And I'm just not sure it's my thing. I mean, I like the attention; I get that it's important in order to get the support we need for the project, but I'm just not feeling this is where I need to be. I've decided I want to go back to New York."

Shannon was shocked. "New York?"

"Oh, come on now. You know I love New York. I always will love New York. I need the city. You don't see me running around here in flip-flops and shorts, and I certainly don't wear a skimpy bathing suit at my age." Rebecca laughed as she named all the things she didn't enjoy about Florida.

"Nor do I," ventured Shannon. "Flip-flops, yes, but a skimpy bathing suit? No, thanks."

"Hanging out at the bar and having older men in their sixties hit on me, drunk and in need of sex, is not my idea of meeting somebody new. I love the city life there. I love the restaurants. Sure, here you have a lot of casual restaurants, but it's just not New York, is it?"

"It definitely is not New York. You've got me there."

"I'm going to head out. And in anticipation of this discussion, I went over all my files with my number two, and I think Connie's going to do a great job in my place, if that's what you decide to do. In any event, she's up to speed. She probably knows some of the things better than I do. She's got a good flare for space and texture and design, and she spends way more time with those SEALs than I do these days, so I think she's a better choice to run your design team."

"I'm really surprised, Rebecca. I thought you wanted to be part of this project."

"Well, that was before we got all this media attention. You forget, I have a past. It kind of follows me around a bit."

Shannon knew what she was talking about. When they'd offered Rebecca to be interviewed, there was a string of reporters who refused to take it due to how she had treated them in the past. She was known to beat up the press, belittling them, and didn't seem to mind the flack she got as a result. As far as being a spokesperson, their PR person, she wasn't really helping the project that much. But still, Shannon was surprised.

"What will you do?" Rebecca gave her a stare like she was made from a pile of rotten banana peels. Shannon corrected herself, sat up straight, and added, "Not that there aren't hundreds and hundreds of jobs you could take, Rebecca. I just mean, what is it that makes you excited about going back there? Surely it must be some kind of job situation or some kind of opportunity."

Rebecca nodded. She finished her coffee, set it down on the saucer, and placed the saucer at the edge of Shannon's desk. Crossing her legs, she folded her hands together. "I'm going to go into the consulting business. Design renovation, that sort of thing. I have a nest egg to work with, and I may even decide to buy and renovate office buildings, office complexes with good bones that need help. Perhaps become a commercial landlord. Or design, fix them up, and sell them. I'm not sure. I could be a consultant for others wanting to spruce up their image or their look. I think I have a taste for that. I'm also hungering to work with other people in business."

Shannon got the implication that perhaps their beachfront-casual company was not really something she enjoyed much. She'd never considered that.

"So do you have some clients in mind?"

"Not yet. I haven't really started putting feelers out. I needed to talk to you first. I want to make sure we're okay, the two of us. Marco and I will never be okay, and I understand he will never trust me, and that's probably a good thing. Given the opportunity, who knows, I might go back to that blood sport."

This alarmed Shannon.

Rebecca must have noticed her change in demeanor.

"Oh, don't get scared, Shannon. I'm just messing with you a little bit. I like fighting. But I like to win if I fight. There is no winning in this game with Marco, only losing. And I have a feeling I would be the one to lose. With you though, it's not a game like that. You've always accepted me straight on, even when everybody else didn't. And I appreciate that."

"Thank you, Rebecca. That's very kind."

"But that can be a flaw. Be careful, Shannon. Don't trust everybody you think you can."

"Are you saying there's something I need to know here?"

"No, nothing of the kind. But your trusting nature makes you naïve. Being naïve sometimes makes you less powerful. I think you're okay with it, because that's not what you seek. You're basically a healer, a support person. You can take the lead, but you prefer to be the one behind the leader, don't you?"

Shannon knew most women would take offense at that comment. She did not. "I think you've got me pegged correctly."

"I, on the other hand, like to be in charge. Running my own company will be a lot more fun than ruining Marco's. I want to make a name for myself on my own. And I think this is a good time; this is my opportunity to do that."

Shannon completely understood and agreed with her.

"I'm going to miss you, Rebecca. I think you're doing the right thing. And I wish you all the success in the world. If there's anything I can do to help you, just let me know."

They both stood, like professional businesswomen, shaking hands—no hugs, no kisses or crying. Just a clean break, a separation, each side maintaining the dignity they'd earned.

And regardless of who got to marry Marco, Shannon knew that both of them loved him dearly.

I truly hope she'll find that special someone like I have.

CHAPTER 13

I WAS AT the jobsite meeting early with several subcontractors. I helped figure out the source of a couple of problems with scheduling. We readjusted two due dates, and then I wrote down the notes so I could update the computer program back at the office. I was scanning the site for the two brothers and came up empty.

Sam was sitting in his wheelchair, talking to two vets who had asked for a little pre-tour.

"Hey, Sam, have you seen Absalom and Khalil yet this morning?"

He straightened himself up in the wheelchair. "No, they were out last night, celebrating. You know that they got the bride-price settled for the girl, right?"

"Yes, I heard that, and I'm relieved it finally happened."

I had wanted them to officially pay the fee demanded when the boys left India with the young dancer. Well, it wasn't really a kidnapping, but they had offered her money to travel with them to the United States from India for a chance at a better life. She was a beautiful, exotic Indian troupe dancer, and Khalil had fallen head over heels in love with her, although there was quite a difference in their ages.

The sultan had been furious with his son but didn't have the heart to separate them. I knew that a bride-price would be requested, and I also knew that, if they didn't accept the terms offered, the boys would be in deep trouble. The sultan could possibly make her go home. Nobody wanted that.

They'd negotiated the deal, and I was under the impression that, with my security detail, they had arranged the payment details. They invited me to the celebration, but I declined. The dancing and drinking until all hours of the morning wasn't something I was really interested in doing.

"So do you think it has to do with that, Marco?"

It hit me that it could be a definite possibility and kicked myself for not thinking about it earlier. Here, we'd just gotten over the sultan's poisoning, and now we might have a situation with his sons. I was sickened at the thought.

"I think that's a bridge too far." But inside, my gut was telling me something else.

I had promised my support and protection and had

five of my best guys on those three, practically shower-ing and sleeping with everybody. They were never to be out of my detail's sight. If something occurred, that meant maybe my guys were in danger as well.

"Have you seen Kurt, Reggie, or Connor?" I asked.

"Nope. But you know, maybe they're just sleeping it off somewhere. They've been late before."

"Yeah, but not after negotiating a bride-price with a bunch of bandits in India. I don't like this. I'm going to call a team meeting. If you hear anything, give me a call please," I asked Sam.

"You got it."

Before I turned to go, I nodded to the two wheel-chaired vets in front of me. "I'm sorry I didn't introduce myself. I'm Marco Gambini, and it will be our pleasure to design you a home far beyond your wildest dreams. That's our mission. Unfortunately, that also means we have to work with a lot of people, and things fall through the cracks occasionally. I'm sure this is just a minor hiccup."

"Before my accident, I worked construction from the time I was about ten," said the younger of the two. He was a bright towhead with big blue eyes. His light complected skin was already getting red from the sun. "I've always wanted to live in Florida. And when I found out about this project, I chose to come down and shack up with my buddy here. And he got me in the door."

"Well, good for you. Good day, gents."

While I was running to my car, I made texts to the detail team without an answer and got on the phone with my head of security.

"I'm getting a bad feeling about Khalil and Absalom being missing this morning from the jobsite. Tell me you know something about it that makes sense," I said to Jeffrey.

"Marco, I wish I did. I know they were partying, and you know how those guys get. But they've been better lately. Have you tried to get the detail team?"

"Yeah, I just tried on my way over here. Nobody is picking up. Where were they last night, do you know?"

"Let's see. I think it was the Blue Crab Grill?"

"Okay, I've got the number. You let me know if you hear anything please, and I want you to call your entire team, put the word out. Anybody knows anything, I want to hear about it right away. Can we meet back at the office in about an hour?"

"You want everybody or just the heads?"

"If they're on assignment, they stay where they are. But they check in with you, okay? Otherwise, I'd like all the heads of your departments who are not assigned. I need some extra eyes and ears, and I need some good ideas and fast. If this breaks into a full-scale hostage situation, I've already lost time."

I called several other team guys and had someone run over to the house Khalil and Absalom lived in, who reported back that it didn't look like anybody had been there since last night. The beds were not made, but the showers were dry. The detail team and their two cars were also gone.

Once I arrived at the office, without greeting anyone, including Shannon, I closed my office door and sat, placing a call to Bonin. My head of security there picked it up before it rang twice.

"Everything okay over there?" I asked him.

"Yep. But that kind of a question means it's not okay over there. Or am I making things up?"

"I can't find Khalil and Absalom. And the three guys I had with them last night are missing as well. I'm fearing something bad. Please tell me I'm being stupid about this."

"No, you're not being stupid about it, Marco. You probably have the best sixth sense of anybody I've ever worked for. But if you're looking for something here that might have spilled over to your part of the world, I don't see it. Everything's been quiet. He's been taking good care of himself. The women seem to be fine, a little quiet too, but busy with the wedding details and attending to their spaces. They have big plans to decorate the great hall, their quarters, the sultan's bedroom, and the honeymoon house."

"Any changes in the staff or anybody being squirrelly? And whatever happened with the kid and Meera?"

"They didn't call you?"

"No, they sure didn't. Who was supposed to call me?"

"Well, the imperial guard in Cochin agreed to place him in a safer prison situation than he normally would've been thrown in. I'm not sure whether it was the sultan's doing or Meera herself pleading for his health. But in any event, the trial was quick, two days, and he was sentenced to twenty years for attempted murder."

"Oh my God, twenty years?"

"Yep. We all expected hanging. I guess the fact that he'd been conscripted to serve in the military saved his life. It's just a guess. You want to know the rest of it?"

"They didn't give time to Meera, did they?"

"It was a shakedown. She was fined, and my understanding is one of the sultan's wives paid the fine."

I knew what that meant. The sultan paid it himself.

"So is she staying in Cochin or going back to her family in Mumbai?"

"She's gone to Mumbai to be with her family, those that are left. I believe she has a job working for a large house."

"As staff?"

"Marco, you know how this goes. She was the wife of the sultan, for a certain period of time, and she did the unthinkable. But the problem, the boy, he's locked up, so there really is no problem anymore. One of the sultan's friends, a wealthy businessman from Mumbai, has taken her into his household, yes, as staff. But I doubt she'll ever have to wash a diaper or clean a window."

Marco knew that's the way it was. No wonder no one from his house informed him of the trial or about Meera. Things were worked out. People didn't talk about it upfront. It was just done as a backroom deal, as a favor, sort of a saving of face. She did pay the price for her indiscretion, although it was slight. She would never be given the kind of responsibility she had at one time or the opportunity. But this assured her that she didn't have to starve or beg or do something awful on the streets of Mumbai. She would've been better off to go to prison than have to do that.

"I want to hear when she's located, okay? And I also would like you to maintain contact with somebody at the prison. I want to make sure that he stays there. It's part of our responsibility with the sultan that if he should ever be let free, we are alerted to it immediately so we can take precautions."

"I understand completely. We will do that."

"Well, I need to go," Marco said as he looked downstairs at the plaza right outside the front doors of the office building. A messenger was bringing a leather pouch into the lobby. He was a private courier service, and he knew that pouch would be searched thoroughly.

"I think I'm about to get some kind of news. I don't think I'm going to like it," said Marco.

"Let's hope and pray you're wrong. But let me know please. If there's anything you want me to do or not do, please tell me."

"You are not to tell the sultan or any of the wives yet. You can tell a few of the trusted team leaders, but no word to any of the staff or the wives or the sultan until I give the okay. Is that understood?"

"Absolutely, sir."

I walked to the doorway, opening it, and watched as the courier made his way through our upstairs lobby quarters, accompanied by my front office receptionist.

"Marco, this gentleman has a special letter that needs to be hand-delivered to you." The attractive older woman had unmistakable worry lines in her forehead, the edges of her eyes squinting, her upper lip curled up slightly in disgust.

"That's okay. Let's give the gentleman a chance to do his duty." I turned to the young man. "What do you have for me?"

"I have a letter, and I need a signature from Marco Gambini."

"That's me. Do you need to see identification?"

"Yes, please."

I reached into my back pocket and produced my Florida license and also showed him my concealed carry permit. "Do you want to see my insurance card, my blood type, or my passport?"

The boy didn't comment, wrote down the number of my driver's license on a clipboard, put an X in a box, and handed it to me. "Sir, if you will sign right there where I've indicated, I will give you the letter."

I did so and was handed the cream-colored expensive stationery I knew didn't come from an office supply store. Then he handed me his business card. The gentleman turned around and my receptionist accompanied him back to the elevator. Once I opened the thick cotton velum, three single lines of typing jumped out at me, with no signature block underneath. I read the lines carefully.

We have Khalil and Absalom.

They are as yet unharmed, but we have three injured security detail who say they work for you.

We will be in touch as to the terms we will require in order to return the two brothers to their father.

I noted they didn't say anything about my security team members.

CHAPTER 14

THE SECOND-FLOOR OFFICE building complex was turned into a command center almost immediately. After having spent years working together, both inside the company and as part of SEAL Team 3 in Marco's early days, the group of men who set things up worked together as one cohesive hive unit. Very little was said. They showed each other certain things as they sat down together at a table to troubleshoot what had to be done. There was the spirit of cooperation and working to connect the cables, to load the data, to print out and analyze the information very quietly. No shouting, no arguing, no bosses, just a group of men working together to put the network in play.

Shannon could see how their SEAL training had created the environment for them to trust each other and learn how to fit in where they could. They didn't have to be perfect at everything, but they learned to fit in and do what they could do without worrying about what they couldn't.

Shannon was stunned at the humility and the lack of confrontation, even though the situation was extremely stressful.

She stayed out of Marco's way, only because she didn't want to distract him. But on several occasions, he came up to her, rubbed her shoulders, or gave her a kiss on the neck, just to let her know he was grateful for her help.

It didn't take long before they identified the players of the kidnap group who had been canvassing the office building, the construction site, and the homes that Khalil and Absalom lived at for several days prior. But they still didn't know who they were.

Marco had tagged the cars and the cell phones of his security team. He also had installed a locator chip in Absalom and Khalil's cell phones. The surveillance cameras outside of their houses were extremely helpful, giving them great facial and physical detail of some of the players.

After pouring over the material, it became obvious to Marco's team that the crew was a hired group of professional mercenaries. Shannon heard the team talking about possibilities, discussing the various groups they'd encountered before, and trying to pin one. Several spoke about how they were an imported group from outside the US, perhaps Russia or China, and that they were expert at hostage removal and negotiation.

"Let's hope they don't know who they're dealing with," Marco whispered over one man's shoulder as they studied a surveillance tape.

One of the men commented, "I've seen these guys before."

"Where?"

"Nigeria. About two years ago. Ruthless guys. Ice water in their veins. Leave a lot of bodies behind. But they are effective through the use of violence and intimidation."

"Sounds like the Wagner Group to me," said another team guy.

"This is a little far for them to travel," mentioned another.

Shannon knew the Wagner Group were paid mercenaries from Russia, war-torn areas of the Eastern Bloc countries, and the worst of the worst from Africa.

Marco paced behind the screens. "Okay, so if we have the Wagner Group, then I need to call Washington."

He grabbed Shannon by the arm and took her into his office, closing the door. "Been wanting to do this all day and just haven't found the time," he said as he kissed her. Shannon was swooning, her knees wobbling from his deep passionate kiss that left her breathless.

He dialed Senator Campbell, who picked up right away. Marco was direct. "So we've got the Wagner Group involved in the kidnapping of the sultan's two sons here in Indian Rocks. I may need some help, and I sure as Hell could use some advice."

"Oh my God, that's not good. I would normally ask how they got into the country, but as we all know, we've got a problem that way. You're by the Gulf, so I'm guessing they might have even made a landing underwater. What do you think, Marco?"

"Yeah, that would be possible. It's also probably a good way to extract. We've been monitoring the surveillance footage we set up. These guys are well-trained, have plenty of sophisticated equipment, and know how to use it. Now my question to you is these guys are hired killers, so if some of them, one of them, two of them, all of them wind up meeting their end, what kind of a problem is that going to be for us? Do I have to capture them or are we licensed to kill?"

"I'm going to have to check on that. My authorization doesn't quite go that high, but I would say definitely if you have to defend yourself or you feel there's an imminent danger to one of your team or to the boys, take your shot. And we'll do the best we can to back you up. What I don't want is some big explosion or firefight in the middle of Crabby Bill's or down at the flea market on a weekend morning, scaring the tourists like crazy. That's what I don't want."

"Understood. I'll keep you informed. We may need some support from the air? Any chance we could get some surveillance pictures? You got any drones flying over here?"

"Think you guys probably have better ones than we do, but I will see if I can arrange some big eyes for you. Any reason to assume this is something other than just a straight hostage situation?"

"You mean like smuggling humans, drugs, or something like that?" Marco asked.

"That's right. Might give our Coasties a little chance to insert themselves if that was the case. Of course, you could always suspect it and then wind up being wrong. That'd be another way to do it, but keep us posted and let me know what you need, and I'll see what I can do. I'll start alerting and setting fires over here."

Marco told Shannon he was very grateful he'd cultivated such a powerful friend, and he hoped that if, unofficially, part of the US government could help back him up, he would have a better chance of pulling this off.

"Have you ever run across these guys before?" she asked.

"Not when I was on the Teams. They weren't created yet. But as a civilian, we have. Sometimes it's hard to tell since they are a secret group and they get in and out quietly, not like a militia group who just shoot and blast their way into an arena." He paused. "How you holding up, sweetheart?"

"Don't think my heart has stopped lobbing inside and outside my chest. Wish I could be as calm as you are. All of you—"

"That's how we do it," he said, brushing across her lips. "Come on. Let's get back and see what they've come up with."

After the surveillance footage was analyzed, one of the technicians determined that the computers Khalil and Absalom had used to communicate with the office had been hacked. An unknown I.P. address had been inserted, which was worrisome, but also gave them an opportunity. First, this indicated their level of skill was higher than they'd expected, but it also gave them an address the team could go after, to trace and perhaps pull that thread to find out information about the enemy.

"They've been watching all of their communications and also the negotiations," someone said to Marco.

Another engineer brought up his theory. "Could just be they wanted to make sure there was no back-channel way they were going to sabotage the money exchange. Maybe they just wanted to confirm the cops weren't involved or the federal government wasn't going to jump in on them? Could be as innocent as that?"

"It could be," Marco sighed. "But we have to assume they have compromising information. We are not doing anything defense-wise luckily, with this project, but we're going to have to break all communication with this office so they don't get access to personal files for any outside jobs we are doing elsewhere in the world. I can't risk our data centers being compromised. And these guys are good at it."

It was added to the to-do list, not something that was going to get the boys back, but it was something they were going to have to deal with after everything either blew up or worked out.

One of the surveillance videos showed two men unloading scuba gear, including rebreathers, leaving the equipment selectively around foliage and sand dunes that edged the Gulf. In the back of the van, they noticed what looked like ammunition and the unmistakable shape of a .50 cal already set up on its stand. That told Marco, and he demonstrated it to the whole team, that loss of life wasn't out of the question for these guys. Perhaps their final farewell parting gift was going to be the elimination of as many people on the team as possible, including the boys.

"How much was the bride-price, Marco?" someone

asked.

Marco asked his head of security to help him out.

"Four million. They brought it in cash and were to deliver it just before they went to dinner. Connor sent me a picture of the drop, and none of the guys who took possession of the cash are in any of this footage. It's another team altogether."

"That makes sense. So they got away with the money, then."

Shannon offered to prepare some coffee, which was welcome. She asked if she should have some food brought in or if they wanted to work straight through. She knew sometimes Marco wouldn't eat for days while he was trying to solve a problem.

The group agreed that an order for food would be fantastic. Shannon took two of the men downstairs to the storage room where they had bottles of water and other supplies, including medical kits, and had them brought up to the second floor, where they also created a quiet room out of one vacant office, adding several cots. Marco had explained people could be taking turns resting and watching until they worked out a solution.

She ordered some pizzas, a bunch of hand-held snacks, and a few sandwiches from a local deli. She was going to go pick them up, but Marco wouldn't allow her to leave the building. It would all be delivered to the downstairs center and received by members of the team.

As the unit pieced together what they could, one by one, little details became clear. The puzzle was being solved. The group determined that all the cell phones had been destroyed at the same time. So there was no back-channel way for them to follow or tag them, and there was no way they could activate the listening devices to hear conversations even while the phone was turned off.

The grounds over at the brothers' houses were searched by another unit of three men, and while sorting through bits of trash and cigarette butts planted around the perimeter, someone found a wrapper from mints at a restaurant. This restaurant overlooked the water in Clearwater, right next to the marina, which was chock-full of huge yachts and motorboats. There was a flotilla or race set up for the weekend, so the area was unusually packed with imported boaters and audience.

"That's a good lead. Go search the restaurant; see if they've seen any of these guys." Marco then sent them photos of various members of the group caught on surveillance video.

Shannon arranged the food on their beautiful con-ference room table, placing the waters out next to a tray with ice. She also made pitchers of ice water as well as two pitchers of iced tea. The blackout shades were pulled so that there would be no lights showing from the outside. They wanted to keep hidden all the activity going on for now to not make themselves a target, unless they already were.

Marco received another call from Senator Campbell and retired to his office to take it.

Shannon walked behind the desks and the monitors, watched telemetry results, heat signatures, and images she wasn't used to seeing. It was an incredible array of equipment. And she had no idea that Marco possessed all these things. She knew everything was stored in the equipment room downstairs, but she had never had an opportunity to see it.

Then she thought about Rebecca and wondered if she'd made it to New York, hoping that somehow she didn't get snagged. She figured Marco wouldn't mind her making the call, but she decided to ask anyway.

"Yeah, you can call her, it's probably what you would've done normally, but just don't tell her anything about this. This information isn't to get outside this room."

"I figured as much. So I'm going to go in my office and do it."

She left the beehive and sat at her own desk after closing the door, relieved to have some peace and quiet at last. Dialing Rebecca's number, Marco's feisty ex picked up on the first ring.

"I hope you haven't changed your mind about letting me go, but you probably know there's nothing you could do to make me stay. Or maybe I'm just being egotistical. How are you doing, Shannon?" Rebecca asked.

Shannon stumbled a bit but managed to get out, "Oh, I'm good. I just wanted to make sure you got to New York and that you're safe."

"I am, and what makes you concerned for my safety? What's going on?"

"Oh, nothing. Well, Marco's working late, and I just thought I'd give you a call and make sure you got there. That's all."

"I'm staying at the Waldorf. It's no secret. If you need to reach me later, and my cell doesn't answer, you can leave a message at the hotel. My rental isn't ready until the end of the month so I'll be staying here a while. I can't wait to get out, walk the streets, and enjoy the sites again. I have to admit I feel a sense of freedom."

"I'm glad."

Relieved that everything appeared to be in order, she decided to make sure the food was fully stocked and asked Marco again if there was anything she could do.

"I think we're going to be here awhile. More coffee. And would you mind whipping up a miracle or two?"

"You think everyone is still alive?"

"For now. When they don't need them is when we start to worry. But we gotta find them first. We're on it."

CHAPTER 15

THE RESTAURANT TURNED out to be just as I'd thought, a really smart tip. Several staffers, recognizing several faces on the videos, indicated there had been a group of men who had dined with them and also took several meals in take-out. One of the staffers recalled two of the group wandered down the plankway of the boat harbor but didn't see if they returned or jumped on board a boat there.

I directed six more assets, who approached the restaurant and harbor, one of them releasing a small, hand-held drone. Marco was pleased with footage that came back. The drone was small and nearly silent, looking like a medium-sized bird as it sailed up and down the pier, taking shots of the interior of several of the larger crafts who might be able to stow away equipment and prisoners. They got several heat signatures, but one nearly forty-foot ocean-worthy yacht showed five stationery figures lying prone. It was impossible to see much detail, but they had five live bodies showing up.

The team at the office went wild.

I directed the team to search the surrounding area, since the harbor was bordered by a City of Clearwater public park, filled with foliage and tall trees casting shadows. We were searching for snipers, extra men tasked with protection of the vessel. We already knew there were two armed men on deck, inside. Time was of the essence, since from afar, the protection team might have been able to see or detect the drone. I was worried they'd get word to the men holding the hostages or, worse, call in a bigger team for defense.

The sky was turning bright rose-orange but was devoid of clouds this night, and as soon as it was dark, we'd hit.

I got word the team had spotted a sniper on top of a building in a small strip mall of boutique shops. He was Target 1. Two others were identified in the park. One was sitting, the other casually jogging but craning his neck toward the boat on too many occasions. He ran past the bench-sitter twice before the team identified him as one of the men loading scuba gear. So he was Target 2. The benchwarmer became Target 3. Another man was identified sitting in a parked car facing the harbor, using a powerful single scope and surveilling the waterway and crafts in front of him.

When he spoke into a collar wire, he became Target 4.

I knew there should be more. Darkness was beginning to descend on the area. The restaurant was closing, and the lights inside were turned off. As the staff left, the team scrutinized the help, matching them to the numbers they knew were there from their visit earlier.

I waited, planning on waiting thirty minutes, which made me nervous as all hell. But then a flashlight was spotted inside the restaurant, coming from the kitchen area, and I knew we had the other man, who apparently had slipped in during their dinner and found a hiding place until closing time.

He was labeled Target 5.

"Draper, you ready at the restaurant?"

"Roger that, sir."

"On my mark, gents. We go in five. Be locked and loaded."

Now was not the time for questions, and I was relieved nobody had one. They knew what to do. Lethal force would only be used if it was necessary. Stealth and silence were our primary goals, eliminating the threat to our team who was going to breach the ship and rescue the hostages.

I felt the command center holding their collective breaths. Shannon sat next to me, handing me a cold water bottle I pushed away. I checked my watch. It was go time.

"On my mark—three, two, one, go."

Instantly, the team acted as one unit. Simultaneously, the benchwarmer, the jogger, and the man in the car were overtaken, each doused with a tranquilizer shot to the neck. The sniper caught wind something was going on, adjusted his site toward the park, and tapped his earpiece just before my man hit the side of his head, shattering the device and probably giving him a nice-sized concussion before he could utter a word.

Draper reported in since we had no visual on him. Target 5 was neutralized.

I ordered the team to breach, and within thirty seconds, a concussive flash device had been lobbed through an open window in the cabin. The two semiconscious guards were also dosed, hogtied, and gagged.

I held my breath as the report came in. Indeed, Absalom, Khalil, and the girl were alive but drugged. They would have to be carried out. On the other side, two of my men remained, both wounded. A third was missing, and my stomach fell to my ankles. I hoped it wasn't the scenario I had envisioned. But until I got proof, I wasn't going to assume anything.

I ordered more assets in, plus the van. The detail were loaded inside, all seven of them headed for the FBI complex in Tampa.

My two men were transported for medical treatment at Morton Plant hospital, one of them being shot. Both had lost a lot of blood.

But the hostages were unharmed, as the caller had said. We needed to find that caller, as perhaps my man's life was at stake.

The brothers and Absalom's four-million-dollar future love-dancer-turned-bride were being escorted back to the office building.

It was too early to celebrate, because we were still down one man with no idea where to search. But, shortly after arriving at the FBI building, one of the men admitted to being a new member of the Wagner Group. In exchange for some kind of deal, he revealed the location of my injured team guy and the caller. I was asked to stand down and allow the FBI to handle the raid, which I had to comply with, but waited with baited breath.

But we were hopeful.

It took over an hour before we got the news that the subject had been placed under FBI custody, and my man had been badly injured and left for dead. He was taken to the Level 1 trauma center at Tampa General and was expected to live.

The cheering started almost immediately after we heard word. I allowed a few moments of mirth to creep into my body before I had the task of making my list of the people I had to call. Of course, Senator Campbell was at the top. I would let my team call first, and then I'd follow up calling the families of my men in the hospital.

Shannon wrapped her arms around me and hugged me from behind.

"You did it, Marco. I got to see it all."

I turned. "No, we did it. I'm nothing without this team. These things never happen like we plan, but we plan every which way from Sunday, and hopefully, it's enough. Tonight, we were lucky."

LUCKY. I KNEW that we'd been lucky. It was all too easy, almost as if it had been a setup. But we had been prepared. We had tripled our security presence, and we had installed surveillance everywhere. I was glad we didn't have to call on the Navy or the Coast Guard or even the local police or Feds, except for detaining the Wagner guys. The State Department was going to be interested in interviewing them, and I knew that they were going to have to be the ones to determine why they got hired and by whom.

But the looming question in my mind was how was this going to affect the sultan, long-term. I began to realize why he hadn't made a big thing about passing on his kingdom to his kids, because now I saw that, although he had been a very powerful ruler and his family unbelievably wealthy for generations, each new generation adding to the wealth of the previous, the world had changed. Even though the sultan had done everything right to protect his legacy, it would not be possible to keep him completely safe. And I didn't like admitting that. Because we weren't talking about somebody's safety on a mission or during a project or a battle. What we were talking about was making sure that wherever they came after the sultan and tried to hit him, that we were prepared. And there was just no fucking way that could happen. The bad guys always had a vote. They always got to change their mind, and they got to act when they felt like it, not when we were ready to take them on.

So I knew it was something I had to discuss with the sultan. And I wasn't necessarily excited about it. I needed to think about it a little bit more.

Maybe he knew this, maybe that's why he invited us to have the wedding at his palace. Perhaps he knew I wasn't going to be able to take on a job like his protection for the rest of his life or to ensure there would be something left for everybody else. I think he understood the impossibility of what he really wanted.

And now, for the first time, I saw it as well.

I'd always thought he'd been too casual about things and too worried about others.

I'd noticed a change in him when I invited him to come to Florida. Ten years ago, when we first began working together, he would've never considered taking a trip like that or walking on the beach with number one, the other wives trailing behind. But he was doing lots of things he didn't used to do. Because he knew he wouldn't be here for the second phase of the operation.

"I'll be God-damned. You son of a bitch. You're smarter than I am, aren't you?" I said.

The imaginary sultan I was talking to laughed in my face.

"Who are you talking to, Marco?" Shannon asked.

"I'm rehearsing a speech. No worries. Hey, listen, I have some calls to make. Can I have a couple of guys take you home? I don't know how long I'll be."

"I'd rather stay."

"The excitement's over. Now comes the paperwork. You don't need to stay for that."

I was lying, of course. But I wanted to be free to express myself to the team and to my callers, and some of what I was going to say, I knew she wouldn't understand.

Shannon agreed.

Before I called the sultan, I dialed Senator Campbell.

"I was relieved to hear it went well, Marco. On the issue of the Wagner Group, it definitely indicates an escalation. I even had a discussion with the Secretary of Defense, and I won't allow this to be quoted, but he seemed to think this was a pre-operational ruse, a foil. He thinks they hired a B team just to see what they'd be experiencing, and when they hire the A team, they'll know better what to do."

Now my apprehension about how we'd been too lucky returned, but there was a valid reason for it.

"What you're saying is this is going to be their plan of attack then? This is going to be how they destabilize certain factions, scare the population?"

"Exactly. They have many ways to get into this country, and we've been advertising it pretty much twenty-four seven in the news. But they can get in by boat, plane, or walk right across the border. They can come from Canada, and they will. The Secretary says he's gotten good intel that small teams are being trained to come in by submarine. They've been spotted all year just far enough off of the coast, primarily the Eastern coast of the United States, where their radar can jam. There are, especially in the Florida coast, so many shipwrecks and coral reefs that they can maneuver undetected if they're small enough. I wish we could've gotten you guys in the water, but I'm sure there will be a next time, Marco. We're still guessing until we have the proof, and we're working on it."

"Hope those B teamers give you good intel. Maybe some of them will fill in the blanks for you."

"Believe me, our guys are going to work these guys

over and get what they can. But he thinks, and I agree, these aren't the top picks. These people were never going to get out alive. They were either going to kill all the hostages and then get killed themselves, or they were going to get captured, and they don't particularly care about them. So they can rot in a cell in Virginia or Kansas or Guantanamo forever."

"Suits me fine."

"Oh, and by the way, we did manage to get the money back. I'm not sure what happens to the bride-price now."

"The girl was frightened to death. I wouldn't be a bit surprised if she wants to go home."

Senator Campbell chuckled. "Well, the United States is a dangerous country, after all, isn't it? That's what they keep saying. Perhaps that's the best solution for everyone. It will break a certain heart, though."

I knew he was right. "So I have to ask some blunt questions, Senator. Is there some kind of favor that the sultan can do for Uncle Sam to perhaps get some protection? I'm trying to wrap my head around how I can keep this from happening again and again and again. He can't even stay holed up on his island. He's so vulnerable. But he's a friend of ours, and is there something he can do to help?"

"Well, we certainly aren't going to fucking put a base on his island, although it's not big enough anyway. I think him being involved in some of the politics in India, with that, he could be our ears to the ground. But, Marco, that's a pipe dream that he can be protected. And I think you better level with the man. He probably already knows it."

"So when I explained to him about these groups and about what's perhaps coming down the line—"

"You do not attribute those to me or to the Secretary, do you understand?"

"Of course. If I explained to him that's our theory, and I explained to him that there is no way anyone can tell him he's safe or his family is safe, then what do I do?"

"I suggest you be prepared for whatever he says. I know you don't want to abandon him. But you can't do this forever, Marco. At some point, you must get off the horse and do something else. I'm wondering if you could ever do that."

"So you're done with me then?"

"Not saying that, Marco. A man has to have a life, you know that."

"And you don't want me to kill myself trying."

"I would never want you to die for Uncle Sam. Why would I want you to die for a sultan in the middle of the Indian Ocean on a tiny island with a pink palace and pink sand beach? That's like what you read in children's books. I'm surprised it's even there anymore."

"So it's up to him then. I just give him the facts, and then he decides what he wants to do."

"That's my advice. It's a free world, not just a free country, with certain exceptions here and there. We have the right to do what we want. We have the right to live, and we have the right to die. Some people think living is more important. Some people think the way you die is the most important."

That sent chills down my spine. I knew men on the Teams who felt that way every time they went out.

"Does this mean you're not coming to the wedding?"

"No, I'm coming. You couldn't keep me away now. But, Marco, you got to figure out when it's time to quit. You got to know that. Otherwise, you might lose something more precious than life itself."

We both said it in unison. "Shannon."

I got home past 10:00, and I was unhappy it was becoming my routine. I knew eventually she was going to say something about it. It didn't matter what I was doing was important. Of course she worried, and a wife *should* worry if they loved their husbands. I didn't want her to. I knew my limits, and I wasn't sure exactly what I could promise. But I could promise to tell her the truth.

I put off my call to the sultan till tomorrow, leaving

a message with their time difference, that I was exhausted and needed to get to bed, and I would make contact with them the next day.

I unlocked our front door, waved to our detail who was just settling in for the night in our driveway, entered our small living room, and looked out through the sliding glass window. The beach beyond was lit by a full moon spilling into the rippling water of the bay, the Gulf of Mexico. I just stood there and watched as the water lapped in the surf, as clouds were strewn about the sky, occasionally covering the full moon. I even heard the cicadas in the distance, screaming so loud that I could hear them through the closed glass door.

This was the place I belonged. This was the magical place I'd always dreamt about. But the more I spent time here, the more I realized that this place wasn't as safe as I thought it was. And that created a dichotomy for me.

While I wasn't going to make that commitment to the sultan, I could make that commitment to Shannon—the commitment to keep her safe forever. That was something I could do and would be willing to risk my life for. But I was done doing that for other people. And although the sultan was my best friend, as close to a father as I could have wanted, he had his own family, and he had his own empire that he needed to watch over. While I might help him, I couldn't do it for him. My responsibility was Shannon. Our life together. The children we hoped to have.

I turned from the window and found Shannon leaning in the doorway of our bedroom. She had on one of those long, silky, black negligees. In the darkness, all I could see was beautiful, smooth skin popping out from it here and there, a long leg, her graceful arms and hands, and one shoulder shone in the moonlight. She was all the things I'd ever wanted in a woman, not only physically but emotionally. Just the right kind of naïve, the right kind of innocence matched with that adventurous and stubborn spirit of hers. And she was so much more. I hoped today hadn't scared her or driven her away.

On my way over to embrace her, I apologized.

"Apology accepted," she quickly answered.

She waited for me to touch her before she spoke again.

"Marco, I missed you. I can't do this without you."

"I understand. And I want to tell you that tonight was just a special thing, but unfortunately, sweetheart, it may happen again. I'm going to try not to make it happen, but it could happen again. I just want you to know I see it, and I will never choose to guard someone else or be someone else's protection at the expense of yours. You must understand that. And I will be doing dangerous things. I'm not ready to give that up."

"I know you aren't. I watched you. I saw it in you. You love it. It's who you are."

I angled my head and chuckled. "Now, I never would've come up with that. Where did you get that idea?"

"Your face. You love what you do. You love putting it on the line. And I love that you love it. But I still miss you. I ache for you. And I think, until you've broken all the bones in your body and you can no longer be mobile, you'll probably be running around shooing people away with your cane or trying to ram some bad guy with your car—maybe running people off the road in your golf cart."

"What did I ever do to deserve you?"

"Well, why don't you step inside here, and I'll tell you a few things about that. No, I'm going to correct myself. I'm going to show you."

"Sounds good to me."

I TELEPHONED THE sultan first thing in the morning. He was irritated I had waited so long to give him the update.

"These are my boys, Marco. I was told everybody came out okay, but these are my boys, and I expected more."

"They could have called you themselves, Sultan, but

I take it, and I accept your criticism. I was exhausted, and I need to have a very frank conversation with you. I'm not looking forward to this."

"Oh, so you and Shannon have decided to go get married in Las Vegas with an Elvis priest, right?"

"That's funny. I would never do that to you. Never, never, never."

"Then what is it?"

"I learned with this last operation that there's no such thing as being completely safe. I think you should actually take some martial arts training, and I think your harem should know how to defend themselves as well. As should your staff. If they're going to be there and protect you when I can't be, that has to happen."

"What are you saying, Marco?"

"I'm saying it's impossible for me to guarantee your safety. I can do it for blocks of time, but I can't watch you and your whole family twenty-four seven. It's just not a possibility. We have to operate in a different fashion to keep you safe. But we can't always be there to defend you. It's indefensible."

"But I pay you to do the impossible."

"And I've been able to do that so far. But we've also been very lucky. As you know, the world is changing."

"So you're telling me you're refusing to work for me then? You've never had problems taking a paycheck before."

I bristled at that a bit.

"It wasn't always for the paycheck. You are my friend, probably my best friend. I realize that. And I'm willing to take on the responsibility of helping get you trained and supplying the men and assets to help keep you safe, but I don't want to promise you I can keep doing this—rescue people or sort out whatever it is that you and your family gets into. This thing with the girl, for instance, and the boat that Absalom and Khalil tried to purchase. You and your family have to start taking some responsibility for this. I cannot do it all."

"You didn't mention the poisoning."

"That comes from a different place. That was a wrong committed against someone else five years ago. You married a young woman to save her, but that woman was what someone else wanted. And think about it, you have more money, you have a big palace, you have wives, you have the perfect life for some."

"So am I to believe that you are quitting?"

"No, I'm not quitting. But I am getting married, and my loyalty to Shannon is going to be first and forever first. And I won't be doing anything that would jeopardize that. So I will help you get as ready as you can, but I cannot do it at the sacrifice of the woman I love."

I was surprised and pleased that it had been that easy to explain my thoughts to him. He seemed to take it well, although with the sultan, I never was sure of what he was thinking.

We still needed to go over the list of suspects, who was the most likely to have launched the attack on the boys, and I knew it would take a while to identify the right person. I hoped the interviews with the FBI were fruitful, but without it, we might never know. I felt good about the fact that I didn't promise something I couldn't deliver. I owed Shannon to give her everything she deserved. She was going to be my main priority.

Working for the sultan was going to give us the money to travel and to experience the whole world. It was my vehicle to the life I wanted to live, not the goal, not the destination.

I was happy with that choice.

CHAPTER 16

SHANNON HAD GROWN up watching old BBC movies, fascinated at following the treks of some of the explorers during the latter part of the 19th century and early 20th century. She loved movies that depicted exotic places and huge expeditions or treks. One of the movies that, of course, was haunting her now was "A Passage to India."

She was reminded of all the helpers, trunks, and luggage and how much of a process it was to travel during those days. She was also reminded of the differences between the classes. There were those who traveled well, those who worked for those who traveled well, and everybody else. Although much had changed and India was now a democracy, there were still old traditions kept, old ways of doing things which would die hard. In short, many people who worked for the sultan, and even the US government, were the lucky ones. They had a steady paycheck and didn't have to worry as much about their future. As long as they did their job, it was a benevolent arrangement.

But it wasn't that way for everybody, and with the wars in Africa and the violence spreading all over the world, it made her realize the time was ripe for mayhem, and she needed to be conscious of it. There wasn't much she could do to solve the problems, but she didn't want to become one of those problems, one of the hostages like the sultan's two sons had been now twice. She didn't want to make people risk their lives to save her, if she could save herself.

She renewed her commitment to herself to learn how to use a variety of weapons and get some martial arts training.

Sitting in the jet terminal in New York, she looked at all the baggage they had brought. And she did feel like one of those women traveling with three or four camels behind them lugging all their possessions. She didn't know why she brought so much, except she had gifts for everybody. She had gifts for wives, children, helpers, servants, and everybody in between. She even had a special gift for the sultan.

"I can't believe you brought so much. You could have just not brought any clothes at all, would've been fine with me." Her husband-to-be was always a prankster.

"I was just thinking the same thing, Marco. But the

reality is two-thirds of these are gifts I'm bringing over from Florida. I have so many people to thank for this wonderful affair."

"Well, you forget, usually people come to a wedding and they bring you gifts."

"You're right. But like you told me the other night, I'm stubborn, aren't I?"

He laughed, and she noticed how visibly relaxed he was, now that they were actually underway. She remembered as a child when her family would go on a camping trip, to Disney World, or to one of the national parks, they were so excited to pack up the car. They had so much stuff they could hardly sit in it. It had been the same when she tried that one year in college. And she sure remembered Em when she had so much in her little car their dad had remarked, as she was pulling out of the driveway, that the rear tires looked like they were flat. He admonished her about getting them checked out at her first gas stop.

It was exciting to be on a great adventure. And she knew it would be. She was glad, because all the problems for not only the project but the safety of the men and women who worked on the project, as well as the sultan's family, were past. But as Marco reminded her, they had to keep ever vigilant. And she sure had learned that one full tilt.

Their jet arrived, and Marco had ordered a larger

one this time. He explained that it was going to remain in Mumbai until they were ready to come home. That way he could have it serviced, have a team who would lock it down and keep it safe for them. He mentioned that it had two bedrooms, but she wasn't worried about that. They only needed one.

"I like your choice today, Marco."

He smiled at her and gave her a wink. "We're still limited staff on board, but I just wanted to be sure you were comfortable, my dear."

"This is a special day. I may wind up sleeping, because I doubt I'll be able to once we get on the island."

"I'd be happy to help you with that, my bride-to-be." He took her hand and kissed her palm, tenderly repeating the movement several times. "Shall we go?"

This was the part in a movie where the orchestra would play. Like the time they went on a helicopter ride in Hawaii with a former Air Force fighter pilot who liked to rock and roll that helicopter like it was his personal warship, they'd risen straight up off the ground. Then, as they had flown slowly over to the canyon, he turned on the "Star Wars" theme full force. Suddenly they had dipped down into the green cut of the lush jungle, and she'd left her stomach on the roof of the copter.

She had never been so scared in her life. Their fearless pilot had been probably the same age as Marco right now, a handsome hunk of a guy with aviators. His white teeth had grinned, especially at her. Em and her mom had seemed to take it all in good stride, but Shannon had been terrified.

Walking across the tarmac, she carried her computer and Marco carried his. They greeted the staff, took their seats inside, and received the briefing from the captain. She immediately slipped off her shoes and tucked them under the seat, preparing for takeoff.

The flight to New York had been choppy, mostly because Marco decided to take a commercial jet, seating them in first class instead of renting one of his planes. He had explained that some of the exclusive behavior that they'd been doing out of Tampa and Clearwater airports might catch the eye of some of the bad guys who were always out there looking for somebody they could fleece, a millionaire they could kidnap, or a wife they could take away and hold for ransom. She was beginning to believe him. At first when he began speaking of it, months ago before they were engaged, she hadn't believed him at all.

They held hands and were given their choice of wine, whiskey, or champagne.

"I'll have champagne," she said.

"And you, sir?"

"I'm going to have some single barrel Jack Daniels. Or do we have any Gentleman Jack on board?"

"For you, Mr. Gambini, we have just about the whole line. Is it Gentleman Jack or is it single barrel?"

Marco looked at Shannon and then said, "Gentleman Jack, please."

He used to be a wine drinker, which was her drink of choice usually. In recent days, he'd taken to purchasing some of the finest whiskey he could buy. Shannon occasionally indulged in that as well.

He expanded his seat to lie back slightly, and they both put their feet together on the leather cushion provided.

"I never thought I would live this way. I never thought I would be going to an exotic island palace. I never thought I'd have Prince Charming sitting next to me, holding my hand, and being, well, charming."

"What did you think of me when you were younger? I know I've probably asked you before but tell me the story again? The story of that day," he asked.

"Of course I was still devastated with Emily's death. And at the funeral, my parents were in complete shock. I knew it was the end of our happy family life as we knew it. Being twelve years old, I was trying to suck it up, but my lower lip was huge, puckering and wobbling, and I couldn't stop sniveling and sneezing, eyes pouring out tears that just would not stop. People kept giving me Kleenexes and handkerchiefs, and I refused all of that help and wiped my face clean with my sleeve.

I got in trouble with my mother for it. My dress was black velvet and brand new for the occasion. But it wasn't an occasion I wanted to be celebrating."

"I get it. Now I understand your expression."

"My expression?"

"You had the look of defiance on you. You were fighting demons way back then."

"I was fighting for my family. I knew so much going to be on my shoulders, because my parents, especially my father, loved Emily so much. I knew I wasn't going to be the substitute he needed. His life was forever going to be a big expansive void. I wasn't going to be able to fill that void ever."

"Perhaps that's not true. You know what they say, circumstances reveal a person. They don't make a person. Maybe that's exactly what you needed to do, which was rise up out of the ashes and be strong. Sometimes we have to change our environment. As a twelve-year-old girl, you didn't have that luxury. So look what you did. You took charge of your life, you went to school, you tried acting and modeling, and you got a job in a place that you love. And look what else happened. Because you made all those choices."

"Okay, so what about you then?"

"I knew I had to get out of that place after I said goodbye. There was nothing for me there."

Her heart jumped with a little pang. Shannon

wanted to tell him, "But I was there, Marco."

She didn't.

"I needed to go be with the guys who would have my back. I needed to risk everything. Maybe I was headed off to battle because I didn't feel like I deserved to live. Em had been begging me to marry before I deployed, and I wanted to have my full concentration on my first tour. And look what happened. I didn't."

"So you weren't conscious of all the people around you, were you?"

"No, that's not true. I looked at your parents, and I saw that they were unreachable. I think even though she was the one who died, I think your father wished it had been me. I had a buddy from the team—"

"Carter, right?"

"That's right. Boy, you have a good memory."

"I met him later, remember?"

"That's right. I forgot about that. Well, anyway I was glad Carter was there, and I knew there was nothing else there for me, except I saw this cute little girl with braces and pigtails standing strong. You looked like your fist would punch me in the nose if I said something wrong, and I thought about what I could possibly tell you that would make you feel better. I was destined to fail at that, but I wanted to try for some reason. It just didn't seem fair, because I knew as soon as I left, nobody was going to be there for you."

She wiped her eyes, as the story was getting to her. She had not heard this part before.

"I looked at the casket and the beautiful pink and white roses that I had sent covering the entire top. The roses were going to wither and die on top of her grave after she was buried there, so I plucked the prettiest bud and brought it over to you, didn't I?"

"You did. That's a memory forever embedded in my brain. There's no way in the world I could ever forget that."

"If you were a boy, I might have given you a memento of my service, but that's not what you wanted. I gave you the prettiest rose, and I told you that I loved your sister with all my heart. And I was telling the truth, Shannon. I think I still love her, and I hope that doesn't upset you."

"No. Of course, I love her as well. I loved my parents even though life with them was changed, and I never really had the relationship I wanted. But that's why I had to come see you, Marco. That man who stood in front of me that day in his white uniform, handsome and tall, the man my sister was going to devote her life to, thought enough of me, a little twelve-year-old girl with braces, to be kind. I had to come see if that was really you or if you were putting on a show."

He wrapped his arm around her shoulder and pulled her to him. "Sweetheart, if this is too painful—"

"No, I'm glad we're talking about it. The only thing that had been unresolved for me until the night we met again and slept together was whether or not you were the real deal. I thought I'd come just to kind of prove that maybe you were some asshole big buff billionaire military man, and perhaps I'd spent my whole teenage and early college years being enamored with somebody who was a fake. I had to find out for myself if that feeling inside my gut that told me you were a man worthy of my love was true or if it was false. And even if I discovered it was false, I had to know that before I could go on with the rest of my life. It sounds stupid, I know—"

Marco reached across, pulled her mouth to his, and planted a deep kiss.

"Always, Shannon. I'll always be here for you. This is how it goes. This is how the fairytale begins. This part here is not imagination." As he nibbled on her lips, he added, "This is real."

They arrived in Mumbai and traveled by limo down to Cochin, there catching Marco's Sikorsky. She was concerned about the luggage, but he informed her that everything had arrived there ahead of them. It had been put on a boat in Mumbai heading straight for the kingdom.

"I hope they have a better track record than the airlines."

"You better believe they do. Their livelihood depends on it."

As they landed, they saw the palace had gone through a huge renovation. Garlands of flowers hung all over the entranceway, and fresh rose petals, which had to have been imported from Europe or a large grower in Mumbai, were laid out across the shell pathway leading to the grand entrance. With the flowers and the rose petals all around, the trees also had been sprayed with rose petals, and in the breeze, it looked like pink snow. It was such a magical wonderland of a place already, Shannon wanted to remember this moment for the rest of her life.

The staff greeted them in brand new uniforms, trimmed in gold, each wearing a significant piece of jewelry, which she took to mean the sultan had been generous. Even the staff's children were present, wearing silks and fineries she had never seen them wear before. Shannon and Marco were greeted like royalty. They could have been the queen and king of England, and they wouldn't have gotten a better reception.

Shannon was having a hard time keeping the tears from running down her face. She kept bowing, placing her hands together, and saying thank you over and over again. She probably said it nearly a hundred times before she got to the front door.

Marco, she could tell, was touched as well. As they entered the great hall, the sultan was waiting for them, standing but leaning slightly against a pillar, which was new. She could see he had some lines on his face and perhaps was experiencing some pain. But nothing would stop him from giving them a grand, wide grin, removing himself from his perch, and coming over to hug them dearly.

"My friends, you honor me with your presence."

Marco grabbed the man, as much to stabilize him as to hug him. "My dear, dear friend. No one in the whole world could ever have done this for us. No one has been more kind, more generous. I am going to be eternally grateful."

The sultan winked and put his finger to his nose. "I'm glad to hear you say that, my pretend son. I want you to think of me until we greet each other someday in another place, in another palace, at another time."

Marco hung on to him, but it was more for the re-action that it caused inside his own body than to stabilize the sultan. He was so moved, she heard him gasp several times, clearing his throat and trying not to let his nose run too much. One of the little girls dressed in a white sari with rose-colored cummerbund brought him a little satin pillow with several pieces of tissue on it. She bowed and handed it up to him.

Someone else had noticed what Shannon had.

They were shown to their quarters after they greeted all the wives, looking as beautiful as they'd ever seen them. The whole banister leading up to the guest room, the room where Marco and Shannon had first loved each other in this palace, was wrapped in garland. The inside of the bedroom was decorated like a forest filled with flowering trees, but the garlands were hand-strung, and they had even brought butterflies into the room so that white-, yellow-, and peach-colored little insects with happy hearts flew everywhere around them. It was a magical touch Shannon didn't think she would ever forget. Where they found so many butterflies, she would never know, but she hoped, in the morning, she would wake up and they'd be all over her.

They embraced and decided they would freshen up and then join everyone downstairs for a toast, which was on the agenda. They had just enough time to tease each other with a nice warm lavender shower but saved the sex for later.

A white sari had been left for Shannon, not one of the ones she had chosen, but all the rest of them were safely folded and tucked into the large cabinet with the carved doors just on the other side of the bedroom. She had some slippers set out that were lined in gold with upturned toes fitting her feet perfectly. She put the silk slip undergarment on and then proceeded to wrap the sari around herself, asking Marco for some help. The white gold-stitched slippers with the curled toes were incredibly soft and comfortable. She applied some jasmine and lavender oils behind her ear, spritzed on some of her favorite perfume, Audrey Hepburn's favorite blend, and looked at herself in the mirror. She gasped as she saw her face.

She was playing "Breakfast at Tiffany's." She was in "A Passage to India." Shannon was a queen in quest for a kingdom. She was a bride waiting for her happily ever after with her Prince Charming. It was all in her imagination, and it lifted her and filled her with unspeakable pleasure.

They went downstairs and celebrated with the small group, and then several of the guests who had arrived earlier began to come in where a large buffet was set. People were informally seated and served. She noted that Dr. Tramel had arrived, alone, as well as several of Marco's men from his security team, all dressed to the nines in white tuxes.

The afternoon and early evening was luscious, and she tried not to drink too much and not to eat too much. Number one wife came over to her, whispering, "So now it is your time, Shannon. We've come to prepare you for tomorrow."

Shannon looked at her with questions in her eyes, then glanced over at Marco talking to the sultan. He'd noticed the conversation and toasted her with his champagne and a wink.

"So this has all been planned then?" Shannon asked her.

"You need to go through the ritual bathing. We will clean your skin, wash your hair, and make you feel beautiful for your day tomorrow. Please allow us this gift."

She had planned on spending a wonderful evening with Marco, but she could see that perhaps that was going to be postponed until the big day. Shannon looked at him as if asking for permission. He nodded and toasted her again.

"Well, then I guess I'm all yours."

She would never forget the way their hands lovingly massaged her and removed just about every hair on her body, which was a little painful at times. Her hair was infused with oils, conditioned, and then shampooed with loving strokes, relaxing her head and neck. Several times during the ritual cleansing, she fell asleep.

They had dipped in the saltwater pool and then the cold pool before the process began. All the wives came in with her, and she appreciated the sisterhood, the laughing, and the camaraderie they had for each other, for their position, for the wonderful life that they had there. She was moved they wanted to share it with her. She was not going to live like this, far from it in fact. But it was a gift they could give her that no one else in the whole world ever could.

Oiled and her hair washed, she was sent upstairs with a special pre-wedding gown and instructed not to have sex with her husband-to-be, which she thought was an unusual request.

As she opened the doors, the butterflies fluttered about her. Marco was sitting under the covers with a light green silk robe on.

"Look at you. You are a vision. How do you feel, sweetheart?"

"I feel like a queen, Marco. But—"

He was up in an instant, taking me in his arms and whispering, "I know, I know. The sultan warned me. Let's dispense with tradition, shall we?"

"Oh, yes, I was hoping you'd say that."

CHAPTER 17

I WAS GLAD that the household staff allowed Shannon and me to sleep in slightly, which was to say we slept until eight o'clock. I brought her coffee in bed, and soon the wives showed up to begin her bridal gown preparations. I excused myself, got quickly dressed, and headed downstairs.

Several new people had arrived either late last night or very early this morning, including Senator Campbell. But we also had the US ambassador to India attend and several other senior State Department officials, as well as most of my team at the office in Indian Rocks. Sam was in attendance as well, telling me he wouldn't have missed it for the world. Several of Shannon's relatives were there, people I had never met before, but sadly, her parents weren't among them.

The house, if it could be called that, was opulently decorated in garlands with flowers and hanging jewels. The rugs were all new, sparkling in their gold and silver threads. The pillars of the great hall were inlaid with lapis and gold, the jewels were polished to a fine patina, chairs were set up in the hall and adorned with white and pink roses. Some of the butterflies from our bedroom must have escaped, because here and there, we would find the happy creatures fluttering over a flower, a fern, or even landing on people's heads. It was quite a conversation starter.

The sultan saw me commenting on the details and took me aside, smiling.

"Look out here. You can see the parrots I brought over."

Through the glass, I saw more than a hundred salmon-and-pink-colored parrots flying around several large banana trees, foraging off the ground and perching on various feeders where some of their favorite delicacies sat.

"You'd be best to stay away from them, however. They are eating much fruit today, especially bananas and figs, their favorite. You do know what happens to the system," the sultan said to me with a wink. "But they are such beautiful creatures, and just like the butterflies, I think they were made out of magic. Don't you?"

"Absolutely, I would've never thought of this. Your imagination is—"

"Oh no, this wasn't me. My wives, they love doing

this. They live for it, I think. But this is a special day, because they honor me by how they honor you."

I made the rounds of several other dignitaries, sat out in the garden with several of our team members, and found a way to ask a few technical questions, but I didn't fill the day with work. I knew we were safely being protected, and probably there would be a video of the entire occasion from many, many different angles, mostly because we had surveillance every place but the honeymoon house. I had strictly given instructions that it not be included in any surveillance other than the outsides.

The group began to gather in the hallway in the great hall. A small trio played ancient instruments in the front of the hall by the altar. The music was unusual, a combination of Indian harp and some unfamiliar reed or flute. It was befitting the great hall and echoed, flowing melodic charm throughout the whole place. I was given the instructions to stand toward the front near the altar on one side, and I noticed the audience was spread out evenly with half of the wives on my side and half of the wives on Shannon's side. The sultan was not there yet as he was going to escort Shannon down the aisle.

One by one, several of the employees and SEAL team members I'd served with agreed to show people to their seats and then joined me. Most of them wore uniforms. However, I chose to wear a white tux. I had the option, of course, but I left the honor to the men who were on active duty.

The harp music began to change pace, and I realized we were getting close to the start of the ceremony. If someone were to ask me if I was nervous, I would say no, but then being perfectly honest, I had as many butterflies in my belly as I saw in the palace.

This was a forever life-changing event, more momentous than anything I'd ever done on the teams or in my business life. It was perhaps the beginning of one story and the end of another. And I was going to move through it with grace and dignity and help my bride in the process. I knew what this meant, that my loyalty would forever be with Shannon.

The music stopped briefly, and then a trio of harpists began a beautiful rendering of a hymn I didn't know the title to. As the audience turned, the vision appeared of the sultan with his fine white tunic, all the medals of his station, the ambassadorships he'd had, the awards he'd received, and one of my tridents I had given him, which technically was a violation but a violation I allowed him graciously.

As the music began, Shannon stepped forward, her white sari highlighting the beautiful curves of her body. Her warm red lips called to me, her smile made me feel like I was riding on a carpet. The wives had done up her hair with braids, interspersed with lace, silk, and flowers. Little pink rosebuds were woven in between as well, perfectly framing her lovely face. Her bouquet was made of pink, white, and cream roses plus several fragrant flowers from the island.

I was transported full circle to the first day I remembered seeing her up close, as I held the rose to her nose and, in my own way, pledged to forever be her warrior prince.

And yet, I didn't realize it until years later.

I gulped in air, watching as she walked carefully next to the sultan, clutching his arm firmly. I suspected perhaps he was doing the same. Both were beaming, nodding to guests along the way as they walked down the gold-threaded carpet to where I was standing. Shannon's delicate scent engulfed me, lighting a fire inside which completely took my breath away. I could hardly speak.

"You are so beautiful. Are you sure I'm good enough?" My voice was scratchy as I tried to force it out so she could hear. I thought I had whispered, but several people in the front rows began to titter.

She gave me a strange look. "Of course you are. You always were, Marco. I will never ever leave you. I will never, ever love anyone as much as I love you. I humbly ask you to forgive all my transgressions, my stubbornness, and—"

I put my hand over her mouth, and again, the front rows began to giggle.

"I will never cause you to want to leave. And I will I protect you until my last breath." I kissed her, and then the reverend we had selected cleared his throat.

That brought us back to real time, and he began the service, reciting an ancient Rumi text on love.

"I choose to love you in silence…

For in silence

I find no rejection,

I choose to love you in loneliness…

For in loneliness no one owns you but me,

I choose to adore you from a distance…

For distance will shield me from pain,

I choose to kiss you in the wind…

For the wind is gentler than my lips.

I choose to hold you

In my dreams…

For in my dreams, you have no end."

The vows were taken, questions asked, and the small personal gifts exchanged, which was their custom. I gave her a small perfect pink shell. She gave me a dark gray pearl.

Our clergy wrapped our hands together in a gold cord, allowed for the preparation and placing of rings. I kissed her palm and then held it to my cheek. I could hear sniffles in the audience, and I knew we were making quite a few people either sad or extremely happy. She kissed her fingertip and then spread it over my lower lip. She took her tears and repeated the motion, which I eagerly tasted.

The reverend announced that we were now joined as one, man and wife, and motioned for me to kiss the bride.

She didn't have time to give her bouquet away, which was what was supposed to happen, so she clutched it at the back of my neck as I grabbed her firmly around the waist and kissed her hard, not letting go, not being appropriate, not holding back at all. She laughed into my ear. It felt so good to feel and touch her in such a happy mood and to hear her joyful sigh.

With my hands on her face and her palms on mine, I said it again, "Forever."

She repeated it to me. "Forever."

We made our way very slowly back down the aisle, hugging guests, taking our time on that long walk back across to the reception area. It was customary for the husband and wife to make one toast and then to disappear, which I was thrilled with.

Two pink crystal goblets were handed to us with pink champagne, and we held them up to the assembly with thanks.

The sultan was the first to speak.

"To romance. To falling in love, living a life of magic and hope forever after. Let us all commit to finding that beautiful place in our lives, where love grows, where all the magic of the world resides."

He turned to us. "To Marco and Shannon, two people joined forever and ever. My dearest friends. May your kingdom last forever."

He raised his glass, and everyone else partook.

I would often remember that day. It was hard to hold it all in my head, but little bits and pieces of it came back to me in the days and weeks that followed. No matter what I was doing, I'd stop to think about how I felt that day, dedicating my life to something and someone new. Dedicated to making myself a better man for it all.

It was as much for the women of the sultan's family as anyone else when they helped Shannon down the pathway, made sure her beautiful sari didn't get snagged in the stones, the shells, or the foliage. We had chosen to walk the mile and a half to the honeymoon house instead of taking the cart, but the cart had been decorated nonetheless, just in case we changed our minds.

At the front door, also adorned with garlands of flowers we knew came from exotic far away locations, a white silk ribbon was cut, and we were, at last, officially on our honeymoon, the doors closing silently behind us.

The candles were scented, infused with scents of vanilla, lavender, citrus, and lime. Some butterflies lingered there. The blue ocean was brighter than I'd remembered seeing before. Night was beginning to form, transforming the whole area into a warm rosy glow.

I took her in my arms and brought her to the bedroom. As we disrobed, the glow of the distant dying sun shone on our faces. I carefully removed the clips and tiny rosebuds and let her hair fall around her shoulders. Without all the adornments, the flowers or the gold threads, with her bare body beneath mine, just the sparkle in her eyes and the ruby redness of her lips were all the garnish that was required.

My life was now perfect. I'd never thought or said that before.

But I now believed in happily ever after.

Thank you for reading Legacy, the last book in the Bone Frog Bachelor series.

If you missed any of the other books that came before, you can find all of them listed here.

https://authorsharonhamilton.com/bone-frog-bachelor/

But wait!

If you're ready to get wet, fall in love with all the men in the SEAL Brotherhood and other series, why not begin at the beginning with the Ultimate SEAL Collection #1 or Ultimate SEAL Collection #2, which contains all the 9 books and two novellas.

All of them are also on audible, narrated by the award-winning actor-narrator, J.D. Hart.

You can find the audio books here.

https://authorsharonhamilton.com/audiobooks/

To download a printable books list, find it here.

https://authorsharonhamilton.com/list-of-sharons-books/

ABOUT THE AUTHOR

NYT and USA/Today Bestselling Author Sharon Hamilton's SEAL Brotherhood series have earned her author rankings of #1 in Romantic Suspense, Military Romance and Contemporary Romance. Her other *Brotherhood* stand-alone series are: Bad Boys of SEAL Team 3, Band of Bachelors, True Blue SEALs, Nashville SEALs, Bone Frog Brotherhood, Sunset SEALs, Bone Frog Bachelor Series and SEAL Brotherhood Legacy Series. She is a contributing author to the very popular Shadow SEALs multi-author series.

Her SEALs and former SEALs have invested in two wineries, a lavender farm and a brewery in Sonoma County, which have become part of the new stories. They also have expanded to include Veteran-benefit projects on the Florida Gulf Coast, as well as projects in Africa and the Maldives. One of the SEAL wives has even launched her own women's fiction series. But old characters, as well as children of these SEAL heroes keep returning to all the newer books.

Sharon also writes sexy paranormals in two series: Golden Vampires of Tuscany and The Guardians.

A lifelong organic vegetable and flower gardener, Sharon and her husband lived for fifty years in the Wine Country of Northern California, where many of her stories take place. Recently, they have moved to the beautiful Gulf Coast of Florida, with stories of shipwrecks, the white sugar-sand beaches of Sunset, Treasure Island and Indian Rocks Beaches.

She loves hearing from fans through her website: authorsharonhamilton.com

Find out more about Sharon, her upcoming releases, appearances and news when you sign up for Sharon's newsletter.

Facebook:
facebook.com/SharonHamiltonAuthor

Twitter:
twitter.com/sharonlhamilton

Pinterest:
pinterest.com/AuthorSharonH

Amazon:
amazon.com/Sharon-Hamilton/e/B004FQQMAC

BookBub:
bookbub.com/authors/sharon-hamilton

Youtube:

youtube.com/channel/UCDInkxXFpXp_4Vnq08ZxMBQ

Soundcloud:

soundcloud.com/sharon-hamilton-1

Sharon Hamilton's Rockin' Romance Readers:

facebook.com/groups/sealteamromance

Sharon Hamilton's Goodreads Group:

goodreads.com/group/show/199125-sharon-hamilton-readers-group

Visit Sharon's Online Store:

sharon-hamilton-author.myshopify.com

Join Sharon's Review Teams:

eBook Reviews:

sharonhamiltonassistant@gmail.com

Audio Reviews:

sharonhamiltonassistant@gmail.com

Life *is one fool thing after another.*
Love *is two fool things after each other.*

REVIEWS

PRAISE FOR THE
GOLDEN VAMPIRES OF TUSCANY SERIES

"Well to say the least I was thoroughly surprise. I have read many Vampire books, from Ann Rice to Kym Grosso and few other Authors, so yes I do like Vampires, not the super scary ones from the old days, but the new ones are far more interesting far more human than one can remember. I found Honeymoon Bite a totally engrossing book, I was not able to put it down, page after page I found delight, love, understanding, well that is until the bad bad Vamp started being really bad. But seeing someone love another person so much that they would do anything to protect them, well that had me going, then well there was more and for a while I thought it was the end of a beautiful love story that spanned not only time but, spanned Italy and California. Won't divulge how it ended, but I did shed a few tears after screaming but Sharon Hamilton did not let me down, she took me on amazing trip that I loved, look forward to reading another Vampire book of hers."

"An excellent paranormal romance that was exciting, romantic, entertaining and very satisfying to read. It had me anticipating what would happen next many times over, so much so I could not put it down and even finished it up in a day. The vampires in this book were different from your average vampire, but I enjoy different variations and changes to the same old stuff. It made for a more unpredictable read and more adventurous to explore! Vampire lovers, any paranormal readers and even those who love the romance genre will enjoy Honeymoon Bite."

"This is the first non-Seal book of this author's I have read and I loved it. There is a cast-like hierarchy in this vampire community with humans at the very bottom and Golden vampires at the top. Lionel is a dark vampire who are servants of the Goldens. Phoebe is a Golden who has not decided if she will remain human or accept the turning to become a vampire. Either way she and Lionel can never be together since it is forbidden.

I enjoyed this story and I am looking forward to the next installment."

"A hauntingly romantic read. Old love lost and new love found. Family, heart, intrigue and vampires. Grabbed my attention and couldn't put down. Would definitely recommend."

PRAISE FOR THE
SEAL BROTHERHOOD SERIES

"Fans of Navy SEAL romance, I found a new author to feed your addiction. Finely written and loaded delicious with moments, Sharon Hamilton's storytelling satisfies like a thick bar of chocolate." —Marliss Melton, bestselling author of the *Team Twelve* Navy SEALs series

"Sharon Hamilton does an EXCELLENT job of fitting all the characters into a brotherhood of SEALS that may not be real but sure makes you feel that you have entered the circle and security of their world. The stories intertwine with each book before…and each book after and THAT is what makes Sharon Hamilton's SEAL Brotherhood Series so very interesting. You won't want to put down ANY of her books and they will keep you reading into the night when you should be sleeping. Start with this book…and you will not want to stop until you've read the whole series and then…you will be waiting for Sharon to write the next one." (5 Star Review)

"Kyle and Christy explode all over the pages in this first book, *[Accidental SEAL]*, in a whole new series of SEALs. If the twist and turns don't get your heart jumping, then maybe the suspense will. This is a must read for those that are looking for love and adventure with a little sloppy love thrown in for good measure." (5 Star Review)

PRAISE FOR THE
BAD BOYS OF SEAL TEAM 3 SERIES

"I love reading this series! Once you start these books, you can hardly put them down. The mix of romance and suspense keeps you turning the pages one right after another! Can't wait until the next book!" (5 Star Review)

"I love all of Sharon's Seal books, but *[SEAL's Code]* may just be her best to date. Danny and Luci's journey is filled with a wonderful insight into the Native American life. It is a love story that will fill you with warmth and contentment. You will enjoy Danny's journey to become a SEAL and his reasons for it. Good job Sharon!" (5 Star Review)

PRAISE FOR THE
BAND OF BACHELORS SERIES

"*[Lucas]* was the first book in the Band of Bachelors series and it was a phenomenal start. I loved how we got to see the other SEALs we all love and we got a look at Lucas and Marcy. They had an instant attraction, and their love was very intense. This book had it all, suspense, steamy romance, humor, everything you want in a riveting, outstanding read. I can't wait to read the next book in this series." (5 Star Review)

PRAISE FOR THE
TRUE BLUE SEALS SERIES

"Keep the tissues box nearby as you read *True Blue SEALs: Zak* by Sharon Hamilton. I imagine more than I wish to that the circumstances surrounding Zak and Amy are all too real for returning military personnel and their families. Ms. Hamilton has put us right in the middle of struggles and successes that these two high school sweethearts endure. I have read several of Sharon Hamilton's military romances but will say this is the most emotionally intense of the ones that I have read. This is a well-written, realistic story with authentic characters that will have you rooting for them and proud of those who serve to keep us safe. This is an author who writes amazing stories that you love and cry with the characters. Fans of Jessica Scott and Marliss Melton will want to add Sharon Hamilton to their list of realistic military romance writers." (5 Star Review)

"Dear FATHER IN HEAVEN,

If I may respectfully say so sometimes you are a strange God. Though you love all mankind,

It seems you have special predilections too.

You seem to love those men who can stand up alone who face impossible odds, Who challenge every bully and every tyrant ~

Those men who know the heat and loneliness of Calvary. Possibly you cherish men of this stamp because you recognize the mark of your only son in them.

Since this unique group of men known as the SEALs know Calvary and suffering, teach them now the mystery of the resurrection ~ that they are inde-structible, that they will live forever because of their deep faith in you.

And when they do come to heaven, may I respect-fully warn you, Dear Father, they also know how to celebrate. So please be ready for them when they insert under your pearly gates.

Bless them, their devoted Families and their Coun-try on this glorious occasion.

We ask this through the merits of your Son, Christ Jesus the Lord, Amen."

By Reverend E.J. McMalhon S.J. LCDR, CHC, USN
Awards Ceremony SEAL Team One
1975 At NAB, Coronado

Made in the USA
Coppell, TX
25 November 2022